GRIZZLE'S
ST ~~GRIZELDA'S~~
SCHOOL
FOR GIRLS,
GREMLINS AND
PESKY GUESTS

STRIPES PUBLISHING
An imprint of the Little Tiger Group
1 Coda Studios, 189 Munster Road,
London SW6 6AW

A paperback original
First published in Great Britain in 2018
Text copyright © Karen McCombie, 2018
Illustrations copyright © Becka Moor, 2018
Cover border pattern © shutterstock.com

ISBN: 978-1-84715-926-7

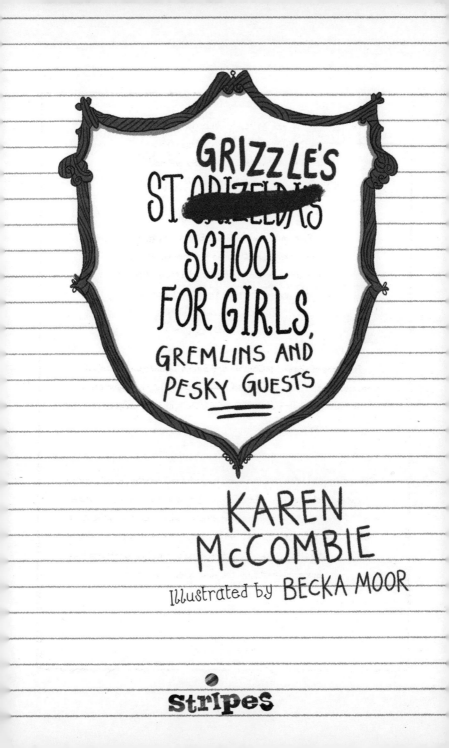

GRIZZLE'S
ST ~~GRIZELDA'S~~
SCHOOL
FOR GIRLS,
GREMLINS AND
PESKY GUESTS

KAREN
McCOMBIE

Illustrated by BECKA MOOR

Stripes

For Mrs Efthymiou (aka Tanya),
one of the legions of tip-top
school librarians out there!
#LoveLibraries #LoveLibrarians

— KMcC

For Callum, Harriet and
the Guinea Pigs

— BM

PROPERTY OF:

ST GRIZZLE'S
SCHOOL FOR GIRLS

Kindly on loan to

NAME	YEAR
Olive Tupple	1919
Augustine Ashburtonshire	1951
Tuesday Smythe-Thrupp	1970
Flora McConk	2014

Chapter 1
Surprises Here - and There!

And SQUEEES
a-plenty...

Once upon quite a while ago, St Grizelda's
School for Girls was, well, just for girls.

But nowadays it's home to **random boys** too.

And I'm explaining all about the *latest* random
boy right at this second.

"SQUEEEEE!"

Wow, that's quite an ear-piercing shriek of
excitement in response to my news. AND it's
coming all the way from the South Pole!

The person *doing* the shrieking is a teeny figure
on the screen of my mobile phone, who is...

a) bundled up in a duvet-sized parka and
wearing chunky goggles, and

b) my very own mum.

"So, quite a surprise, right?" I say, smiling at
the screen even though I've just leant in
something gloopy on the sticky-from-breakfast
table in St Grizzle's dining hall.

"Hi, Mrs Dexter!" says my best friend Arch,
leaning in beside me and waving at Mum.

"So, Arch Kaminsky, you're a Fungi now, are you?" Mum laughs.

She's not being rude – since Arch is eleven, he's in Fungi Class, along with me and sweet 'n' shy Zed (the OTHER random boy at St Grizzle's). Not forgetting Zed's definitely-NOT-sweet-'n'-shy twin sister Swan, of course (I wouldn't dare).

"Yep," says Arch. "Dani was missing me SO much, she BEGGED me to come!"

Well, that's not **exactly** true, but I'm still super-glad my best buddy is here.

"I can't believe it!" says Mum, slapping a fat padded glove to her forehead with a dull flump. "First, your gran and Downboy turn up, Dani, and now Arch?"

When my zoologist mum dumped me here and went off on a three-month penguin-studying expedition to Antarctica I was in a **VERY BAD MOOD INDEED**. I didn't want to go to a stupid boarding school. I didn't want to be apart from Arch. I didn't want to be away from my excellently mad Granny Viv or my daft dog Downboy.

But the thing is, there's a real shortage of staff at St Grizzle's, so when Granny Viv got caught spying on me ("CHECKING on you, darling!") head teacher Lulu ended up offering her the job of live-in cook, homework-helper, bedtime story teller and whatever-else-er-er … and Downboy came too.

Speaking of shortages, there aren't too many

pupils here either, so when Arch turned up out of the blue there was no problem with him becoming a temporary student.

"Oh, hello ... who's this?" Mum suddenly asks, leaning in a little closer to her propped-up phone.

I spin round, thinking it's probably Twinkle the school goat meandering by – but it's not, it's the New Girl. She started at St Grizzle's last week, same as Arch. However, she DID get dropped off in a posh car by her parents. Arch ... well, he turned up via three buses, a trudge through a marsh, a short-but-frantic chase by a cow and a tight squeeze though a spike-tastically thorny hedge.

"**Boo!**" says the New Girl, in response to Mum's question.

Mum's furry hood tips to one side as she wonders why a small stranger 10,000 miles away might be trying to make her jump.

"Mum, this is Boudicca Featherton-Snipe,"

I explain. "Only she likes to be called B—"

"SQUEEEEE!"

OK, so that's **NOT** Mum shrieking this time – it's *Boo* who's burst my eardrum.

"Ha! NO WAY! Check it out, Dani!" roars Arch, pointing at the phone screen.

Uh-oh ... the view of Mum has been blocked on HER side by a large, looming, black-and-white head and a pair of circular, staring, yellow eyes.

"PENGUIN!" yelps Boo, who is crazy for anything winged and feathered.

"Oi!" I hear Mum shout, as the bird starts **clunking** on her phone's screen with its beak. "Leave that alone, you nosey old—"

The screen goes blank as the connection is lost.

Uh-oh.

Seems like Mum has been the victim of a fishy-breathed mobile-phone mugger...

Chapter 2
Numpties and Hurumphs

And the loo-roll fight...

"*Please* make it work again, Dani!" Boo urges, as I try to reconnect with Mum. "I want to see the penguin!"

"Yeah, and I want to see my mum," I say, clicking, waiting ... and imagining Mum lolloping across banks of snow after a speedily waddling penguin, trying to barter a nice fresh sardine in exchange for her smartphone.

A few minutes and a few re-tries later, I sigh and give up.

"So, what'll we do now? What happens around here on Sundays?" asks Arch, looking at me hopefully, just like Downboy does when he wants a walk, or half my toast.

Boo blinks at me, too, but then again she does everything that Arch does. Eight-year-old Boo instantly bonded to my best friend the way orphan animals do in YouTube clips. You know – a dainty baby deer who's being brought up by a baboon, or some diddly little ducklings snuggling with an aardvark or something.

Yesterday, Boo even copied Arch's hairstyle by chopping off her mega-mega-long hair.

"Sunday's when most people check in with their parents, depending on which country and time zone they're in," I tell Arch.

This morning I narrowly missed being splatted by Klara, who was cartwheeling down the corridor yelling to her parents in German, "Mutti! Vati! Schau, was ich tun kann!" while her classmate Yas filmed her.

And straight after breakfast, Angel Skyped her mum and dad on the set of their latest Bollywood film in Mumbai. They must be giving her a sneak preview of the movie – bouncy Bhangra music is still ra-da-da-da-DA-ing along the corridor...

But at the mention of parents, Arch wrinkles his nose. Right now he's not a big fan of his OWN mum and dad, because they've just announced they're splitting up. It's why he did the stupidest, riskiest thing EVER and ran away from home to come and see me. Luckily for Arch, the worst that happened to him on the way here was getting attacked by prickly shrubs.

I notice Boo's got an equally wrinkly nose and it's not just cos she's copying Arch. Her parents aren't exactly warm and cuddly types, so Boo's probably dreading her OWN catch-up phone call – it's bound to be about how many hours' homework and violin practice she's done, and if she's remembering to brush her mega-mega-long hair a hundred times a day. (Oops...)

"Hey, you guys," says Swan, suddenly swinging around the doorframe of the dining room while blowing a giant bubble of pink gum. "Lulu's back from the village with the shopping – we need to help her unload."

Don't think I'll ever get used to the fact that Swan and Zed call their mum by her first name, I think to myself, as we follow Swan into the huge, dark-panelled entrance hall and out of the grand double doors into the sunshine. The school minibus is parked on the driveway next to Daisy (Granny Viv's camper van) and the stone statue of St Grizelda (who's wearing gardening gloves this morning and has a yellow party tooter taped to her grey lips).

"There!" says Lulu, piling family-sized packs of toilet roll on to Zed's lap while her daughter pads across to them. We hear Swan **POP!** her gum in surprise as she's divebombed by a passing pigeon.

"Marvin!" Boo calls out, so pleased to see her feathery best friend that she skips off after him.

"Cute, huh?" I turn to say to Arch – just as a toilet roll bounces off Arch's forehead.

"Oi! You were meant to catch that, you numpty!" Zed calls out as he speeds towards the school building in his wheelchair.

"Yeah? Well, we'll soon see who's the numpty!" Arch yells back, scooping the unravelling missile off the ground and aiming it at the teetering pile of toilet rolls on Zed's lap. "Ha ha ha! Bullseye!"

"Aw, man! Why'd you do that?" groans Zed, struggling to catch the tumbling packs.

"Loser! Loser!" Arch chants, so busy doing a victory dance that he doesn't see Zed sneakily taking aim again. "**Oof**...!"

I walk past them, **tsk**ing and rolling my eyes at their daftness – till I spot that Boo is watching their exchange with a worried expression, as well as a pigeon on her shoulder.

"Why are they being so horrible to each other, Dani?" she squeaks in a scared little voice.

"Oh, don't worry – they're fine," I try to reassure her.

"Honest?" asks a clearly stunned Boo.

Because she's an only child who's been home-schooled till now, I guess Boo has no idea how boys work. Or girls, for that matter. Boo's only friend in her lonely big house was the cooing pigeon that's now gently pecking at her shorn tufts of hair. And she had to keep Marvin secret, since her parents are the complete opposite of animal (and bird) friendly.

"Honest," I carry on as I steer Boo towards the minibus. "Bantering, mucking about—"

"Thumping each other," Swan joins in as she passes us, swinging a couple of shopping bags. "It's how boys show they like each other. The big idiots."

"You know, I think I'm quite glad there are only two boys at St Grizzle's…" Boo says thoughtfully, glancing back at the sniggering, play-fighting Zed and Arch over the shoulder that *doesn't* have a pigeon on it.

"You can say that again," I agree. "I'd rather have a whole **herd** of goats than any more boys!"

"Who's heard what?" Lulu asks brightly, having mistaken what I said just now. "Oh, whoops… Can you catch that, Dani?"

Quickly, I stamp my foot on a drifting piece of printed paper that's fluttered out of a shopping bag.

"There you go," I say, picking it up and passing it back to Lulu.

"Thanks!" she says, stuffing the slightly crumpled sheet into her pocket while slamming the door of the minibus shut. "It's a flyer I was handed at the supermarket – seems the village school are holding a fundraising fair this afternoon."

"Hurumph!"

Whoops – the snort comes out of my mouth without it meaning to.

"Ooh, that didn't sound like a very positive noise, Dani!" Lulu says with a mix-up of a frown and a smile. "Not a fan of school fairs?"

"Just not a fan of the kids at the village school," I tell her, thinking I might as well.

"Ah, yes, Swan and Zed *have* said something in the past about them not being very friendly, which is a pity," Lulu says with a sorry-sort-of-sigh.

"It's more than not being friendly," I grumble. "They're pretty rude to us, too."

"Oh dear!" Lulu frowns. "What, ALL of them?"

I think for a second and realize that's not *exactly* true. There's one particular group – and one particular ringleader – that's guilty of the rudeness.

"Well, most of them tend to **stare** and **not smile**," I reply, thinking back to the times I've seen the local kids in the village, or during the schools' film awards a couple of weeks' back. "But there's this one boy, Spencer, and his mates who always give us a hard time."

"Really?" says Lulu. "What sort of things do they do exactly?"

"Oh, just dumb, name-calling stuff," I reply, realizing I don't want to spoil a nice morning by thinking too much about an idiot like sneery Spencer.

"Hmm, we'll have to do something about *that*,"

Lulu says thoughtfully. "And I have JUST the idea..."

An idea?

To do with Spencer and how to get back at him?

Yesss!

And then I look at Lulu's kind and trusting face – lit up with a sparkly smile – and realize this 'something' of hers, it *isn't* about getting revenge, is it?

OK, so now I'm beginning to worry **big-time**...

Chapter 3
No-fun Numpties

And the village school fair...

Tinkle-inkle-inkle ink!

It sounds as if St Grizzle's really *does* have its own herd of goats.

Blossom's dad – a soldier stationed in Afghanistan – posted her a package of trinkets he'd bought at a local market. Inside were heaps of bell-covered anklets and bracelets – enough for Blossom and all her Newts classmates. They're all merrily jingling and jangling as we pass the sign that says...

'WELCOME TO HUDDLETON'

...and head into the village and down a side street.

Up at the **head** of the straggly crocodile of St Grizzle's students is Lulu, holding Twinkle and Downboy by their leads. She turns round to nod at Granny Viv at the **tail** end of the crocodile and they give each other a quick thumbs up, which is the international teacher signal for 'Phew, we haven't lost any kids so far.'

In between Lulu and Granny Viv, the rest of the crocodile looks like this...

• **Newts Class** (all ten of them), with teachers Miss Amethyst and Mademoiselle Fabienne shepherding our sound-a-like goats.

• **Otters Class**, who are nine-year-old triplets Tia, Tiane and Tineesha. Japanese student Toshio – the school's temporary receptionist – is 'in charge' of the three sisters, which seems to mean listening to music on his chunky headphones and sharing his Tic-Tacs with them.

• **Conkers Class**, ie ten-year-olds Angel, May-Belle, Yas (all chatting) and Klara (sulking, as she's been banned from cartwheeling on a main road).

• **Fungi Class**, which is, of course, me, Swan, Zed and Arch ... with little, tag-along Boo.

"Must be nearly there," says Granny Viv, as we hear the unmistakable sound of laughing, roaring and music that has to mean we're close to the village school and the fair.

In next to no time we're walking alongside railings looped with colourful, flip-flapping bunting, and straight away spot the playground packed with rickety stalls and milling people. The boxy school buildings are as modern-looking as St Grizzle's is old-fashioned, but like ours, it's in a nice setting – St Grizzle's has woods wrapped around it, while the village school has the river practically lapping right up to its doorstep.

"This is a totally rubbish idea of Lulu's," Swan says with a sigh, before blowing and **POP!**ing a pink bubble of gum.

"Yeah, Swan, but you know Lulu thinks us coming today will help," Zed adds in their mum's defence. "She's hoping it'll mean everyone in the two schools will become friendlier."

"Yeah, like THAT'LL happen," Swan growls. "Check out the looks we're getting already!"

Uh-oh, Swan's right. Even with all the bustle and noise going on in the playground, smile-free faces have begun to turn towards us, stares are being stared. Gulp. I reach for Boo's hand so she doesn't feel nervous. But then maybe it's the other way around.

"Ha! Of COURSE people are looking," Granny Viv says breezily, as our crocodile comes to a standstill in front of the open school gates. "With all the tinkling going on, they probably think Santa's sleigh is on its way. They're just curious. Well, except for THAT bunch of scowlers…"

WELCOME TO TWITTERING

COCONUT SHY

Ah, no surprise that the 'bunch of scowlers' Granny Viv has nodded towards is Spencer and his cronies – three boys plus one girl. They're hovering by a coconut shy, switching on their very best sneers as they spy us coming. Granny Viv is no fan of Spencer's. When he was rude to her on a shopping trip to the village, she got her own back by photo-bombing a film project he and his classmates were doing for a local schools' competition. (Go, Granny Viv!)

"What's *their* problem?" says Arch.

"Us," says Swan with a weary sigh.

"See the sneeriest one, in the middle, with the stupid big blond quiff?" I whisper to my best friend. "That's Spencer – the boy I've moaned to you about."

On the right of Spencer is a tall boy with even taller hair, and then there's a guy with dark, curly hair whose jaw drops and whirls around in a circle as he chews gum, making him look a bit like a really mean cow. On the left is the girl, with her face all pinched like she's just stepped on a drawing pin.

"Huh, well, him and his mates look like no-fun numpties to me," Arch announces, summing up Spencer and his crew pretty perfectly, I think.

As we get closer to the entrance, all four no-fun numpties cross their arms and look plain cross, making it obvious that they'd like it VERY much if the smiley lady selling tickets at the gate told Lulu she'd run out.

But tough for them – the smiley lady is taking money from Lulu and giving her a clinking handful of change with an extra-wide smile.

"Yoo-hoo! Spencie, sweetheart!" The lady turns round and calls to a startled Spencer. "Can you do Mummy a favour? I've run out of coins… Can you grab me some more from the Soft Toy Tombola so I have enough for the next customer?"

"Yes, Mum…" Spencer mumbles darkly, as he walks over and snatches the twenty-pound note she's wiggling at him. He goes to slouch off, but his mum has other ideas.

"Oh, Spencie, sweetie, can you take Katniss with you? Just till I finish my shift, darling?" she asks, pointing to a chubby baby in a buggy, who's holding an ice-cream cone in her pudgy fingers.

With a grunt and a groan, Spencer grabs the handles of the buggy and trundles off, nodding at his mates to follow him. They all try to swagger, but it's kind of hard to look like a cool crew when you're pushing a small kid that's mostly covered in ice cream.

And that's the reason a giggle wriggles in my chest – and bursts out, too loud.

Spencer gives me an 'I'll-get-you-back' glower over his shoulder in return... Gulp.

"Gather round, everyone!" Lulu suddenly calls out, ushering us into a half-circle huddle.

With some shuffling and tinkling, we do.

"Now, you've all got your pocket money, haven't you?" she asks.

Lots of heads nod and things jangle.

"Good. Well, I want you all to have LOTS of fun at the fair," she tells her St Grizzle's brood, "but remember, I DO expect you all to be on you very best behav—"

Lulu doesn't get to finish her sentence.

"BOUNCY SLIDE!" yells Blossom.

The answering "**YAAAAAAaaaayyyyy**"s fade as the rest of the Newts stampede after her, all headed for a giant inflatable that's wobbling like a primary-coloured rubber jelly in the far corner of the playground.

Lulu puts her hands on her hips, rolls her eyes and laughs.

"Well, fingers crossed those girls don't wreck the school!" she jokes.

Lulu doesn't notice the person who's strutted up beside her – but WE all do. He's the village school's head teacher – we saw him at an award ceremony at the town hall recently, where all the schools' short films were shown.

"Ooh, Mr Puddock, isn't it?" Miss Amethyst says politely to the stern-looking man in a grey suit and stripy tie. He's not that old but his short hair is steely grey as well.

He stares at Miss Amethyst's fluff of mauve hair and then lets his eyes drift disapprovingly to the flowery garland that sits daintily on Mademoiselle Fabienne's head.

Next, he wordlessly stares at Lulu's newest and cleanest T-shirt (it has a happy dolphin on it and the word 'Yippee!') and finally frowns down at Twinkle, who is eating the macaroni-and-string necklace that the triplets made and hung round her neck.

Even Mr Puddock's **stare** is grey.

"Who is this guy?" Arch whispers.

"Head teacher here at Twittering," Zed whispers back.

"Twittering?!" both me and Arch hiss at the silly-sounding name.

I even hear Granny Viv snigger beside me.

"I didn't know that was the name of the village school!" I say, gazing around. Sure enough, '**TWITTERING PRIMARY SCHOOL**' signs are littered all over the place. "I thought it would be Huddleton, same as the village..."

How did I miss noticing the name during the recent schools' film awards ceremony? I guess it was all so busy that day, and I was too focused on our film.

"Think it was called after some super-posh lord who lived around here, like centuries ago or something," Swan mutters.

"Twittering," I repeat silently to myself, as I watch Lulu flick on her sparkliest smile and beam it at the grey man standing beside her.

"Nice to see you again, Mr Puddock," she says cheerily. "Haven't seen you since that last head-teachers' conference!"

"Ah, yes, Ms Murphy," the other head answers dryly.

"Oh, please, call me Lulu. Everyone does," she insists. "Even my own children!"

Mr Puddock pulls some muscles in his face that I *think* were supposed to result in a smile, but it doesn't really work out that way.

"The conference..." he carries on, without responding to what Lulu just said. "Wasn't that when you announced you were going to radically change the style of St Grizelda's, Ms Murphy? To make it more 'fun'? And am I right in thinking it was fairly soon **after** that most of your students and teachers left?"

Lulu's smile falters a little.

I can hear a low growl coming from close by and I know by the tone that it's NOT Downboy. This Mr Puddock better watch out – Swan can be pretty fierce when riled.

"Well, change is never easy for everyone," Lulu

says after a moment.

I think we all take a quick peek at Yas right then – she's the only pupil at St Grizelda's who still wears the old uniform, and who has her suitcase permanently packed and ready for when her father comes to pick her up. (He hasn't yet. And despite saying she thinks the new version of St Grizzle's is silly, she seems to be having a pretty good time.)

"So … at the conference, didn't you mention some building work you were having done here, Mr Puddock?" asks Lulu, trying to get the conversation back on track.

"Yes, indeed," says the other head, instantly preening like a peacock. A grey one. "As you can see, our brand-new extension has just been completed."

Along with the adults, me, Zed, Swan and Arch glance over at a fancy, glassy building that's close to the river. But all the head-teacherly talking has instantly **bored** the Otters and Conkers, who've quietly peeled away to go and explore the fun-ness of the fair. From my now-empty hand, I realize even BOO has bumbled off.

"Actually, our **extraordinarily** talented Year 6s have been hard at work rehearsing in our new hall with its state-of-the-art drama facilities," Mr Puddock carries on with his boasting. "They're performing a rather fantastic show here on Tuesday evening."

"Really?" says Lulu, sounding genuinely interested. "What's the show? We'd love to come and watch!"

"Oh, **no**!" Mr Puddock replies too quickly, wrinkling his nose at that plainly horrible suggestion. "It's a show *just* for the elderly residents of the old folks' home. They're SO looking forward to it, the poor souls, and SO grateful to us for—"

PARP! PARP!

Mr Puddock nearly jumps out of his suit as a man on a mobility scooter screeches to a stop beside him. The man is quite a bit older than Granny Viv. He has a tweedy trilby hat perched on his head and a little, frizzly goatee beard.

"Oh, this is Mr Scott!" Mr Puddock pants, as he tries to gather himself together again. "One of the residents of the old folks' home I was telling you about."

"The name's **Neville**," the older man corrects him. "And it's NOT an 'old folks' home' … it's the Huddleton Retirement Lodge. Anyway, what's going on with the barbecue, man? They've run out of hot dogs already! AND there's no more ketchup. There's practically a *riot* going on over there, I tell you."

"Oh. Um, I'd better see what's going on. Please excuse me, Ms Murphy," Mr Puddock mutters, marching off to sort out the barbecue disaster.

After watching the head teacher leave, Neville aims a cheeky wink our way, tips his hat at Twinkle, then zips off sharpish on his scooter with a friendly **PARP! PARP!**

"Thank goodness for Neville!" says Granny Viv. "I thought that *awful* Mr Puddock would drone on forever!"

For a second, I think Lulu is about to tell Granny Viv off for talking rudely about her fellow head teacher, but I can see a hint of a smile at the corner of her lips.

All she DOES say is, "Right, I think we deserve to have a good time now, don't you…?"

Lulu doesn't need to tell us twice.

While the adults drift away with Twinkle and Downboy, Arch grabs the handles of Zed's chair and zigzags him off through the crowds at high speed.

Swan hurries after the two laughing boys, but I hesitate, all of a sudden sensing a **wibble** in my tummy.

A **wibble of worry**.

A **wibble of worry** about Spencer and what he might do to get back at me. I mean, he's *never* going to forgive me for giggling at the 'uncool' sight of him being stuck with an ickle baby and a buggy, is he…?

Chapter 4
Say No to Splats

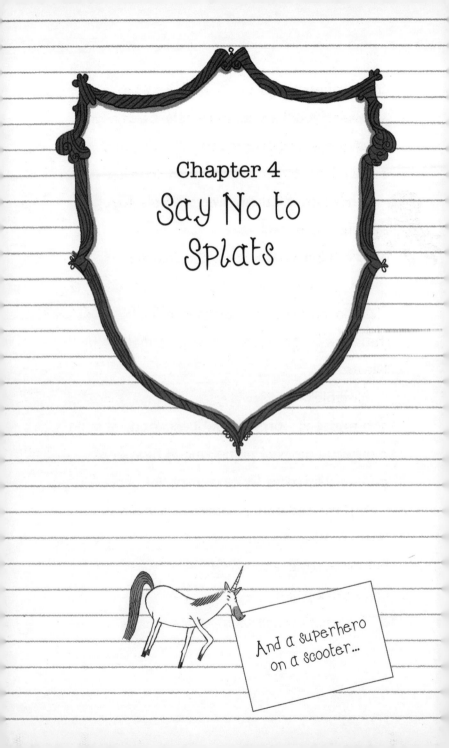

And a superhero on a scooter...

"Aw ... these are going to look SO cutsie-wutsie on your bed, baby brother!" Swan says sarcastically, staring down at the pile of teddies and assorted etceteras in Zed's lap.

He just won them all on the **Soft Toy Tombola.**

"First, you're only older than me by about one-and-a-half seconds," Zed reminds his twin. "And second, you *know* I'm giving them all to the Newts."

Hmm. Like the Newts really need any more soft toys. Their dorm is mostly made up of mountain ranges of furry snugglies and a sea of unwashed socks.

Still, me and Arch could take a few off his hands for the mini-movies we like to make. ALL our mini-movie actors are ex-toys of ours, or charity-shop finds.

"So, what'll we do next?" asks Arch.

He's rubbing a hand on his face as he talks, as if he's lost in thought. But really, he's just showing off his accidental manicure. Earlier, he went to the **Face Painting Stall** cos he wanted to get made up as Spiderman for a laugh. But he got in the wrong queue and ended up with his nails being varnished neon-yellow with glitter highlights by an enthusiastic six-year-old girl.

"We've done everything, haven't we?" says Swan, drawing a finger down the list of activities on a flyer we were handed when we arrived.

We've certainly done lots. In the last twenty minutes, me, Swan, Zed and Arch have tried out stuff like...

- the **Raffle**, cos we all wanted to win the

chocolate hamper (instead we won a pair of men's hiking socks, a giant plastic pen that doesn't work, a voucher for a foot massage with *fish* and a second-hand CD of opera songs that has no CD inside the case)

• **Picking the Zombie's Brain**, where we took turns to put our hands in a giant vat of cold spaghetti to win tiny plastic prizes

• **Hook a Duck** – till a Twittering kid hooked the side of the paddling pool and burst it, and

• **Guess How Many Marbles Are in the Jar**, which went fine till a runaway goat (ahem) knocked over the table holding the jar. Luckily the very nice man running it quickly turned it into a **Who Can Collect the Most Marbles** game and the chaos was tidied up pretty speedily.

"Hold on…" says Swan, her finger stopping at something. "We've missed the **Splat Stall**!"

"Yeah? Where's that, then?" I ask, gazing around.

"The **Splat Stall**'s round the corner!" says a passing small, very wet kid, who must've overheard us. He's with a totally dry kid. "It's ACE!"

"Er, OK," says Zed. "So, what happens at the **Splat Stall**?"

"One of you wears this sort of TARGET," says the wet kid, "and your friend chucks soaking sponges at it."

"Yeah, but sometimes you MISS the target," the dry kid butts in. "On PURPOSE!"

They both cackle madly and mooch off, leaving the four of us grinning at each other.

"Up for it?" says Arch, as we all speed towards the corner of the building and the dumb-but-fun-sounding game just beyond.

"It's me and you first, Arch," Swan challenges my best friend. "You're wearing the target and I am going to *take you down*!"

"Oh, yeah?" says Arch. "Bet you couldn't hit a

target if you tried, Swan."

"Exactly!" she replies smartly, narrowing her eyes at him. "That's my plan, you doughball!"

We're all laughing – till we aren't.

Cos as soon as we turn the corner we see something that makes us stop in our tracks.

Standing on a box is a smallish kid, wearing a sort of round sandwich board with a target painted on it. Her skinny legs and knobbly knees are visible underneath it. Her narrow face, with wide eyes and a hopeful, nervous smile peeks above it.

It's Boo.

And a few metres away from her are several yellow buckets filled with cold water. The trouble is, there's not just ONE kid armed and ready with a sopping-wet sponge to fling at her – there's FOUR.

And they are sneery Spencer and his numpty mates. Spencer spots me out of the corner of his eye and his sneer switches to a nasty smirk.

So is THIS how he's getting me back for laughing at him earlier? By finding the teeniest and most trusting of my St Grizzle's schoolmates and ganging up on her?

"Stop RIGHT there – you hear me?! RIGHT NOW."

It's not me shouting out, or Swan, or Zed, or Arch, though all of us were about to.

The voice doing the shouting is deep and gruff, and it immediately makes Spencer and co turn round, lowering and letting go of their dripping sponges.

48

The voice belongs to Neville, who has come zipping around the corner of the building to help Boo – the first-ever superhero on a motorized scooter.

"What d'you think you were doing, all of you big children picking on a little girl?" Neville growls, as he steers himself over to Boo.

"SHE agreed to it!" Spencer retorts, pointing his arm in the direction of our small classmate.

"They said it would be fun," squeaks Boo, as Neville tries to wrestle the weighty target off her. "But with them all lined up like that ... it didn't seem very fun after all."

"You think it's OK to be mean, do you?" Swan snarls at Spencer.

"Yeah, I call it BULLYING!" shouts Arch, with pink peaks of anger on his cheeks.

"It's no big deal," Spencer snaps in reply. "Can't any of you Grizzlers take a joke?"

Suddenly I see red.

And suddenly, I remember the name of this school: Twittering.

"Think scaring her was funny, do you?" I dive in. "Well, Spencer, if *we're* Grizzlers, then *you* lot are TWITS. And the name SO suits you. **TWITS, TWITS, TWITS!**"

Swan, Zed and Arch pick up the chant, much to the surprise and irritation of Spencer and his mates. And it's not ONLY us … more voices suddenly join in. Running round the corner are a herd of jingling, jangling Newts, who must've seen what was going on from a distance. Before Spencer and his idiot friends know what's hit them, ten fierce girls are pelting them with wet sponges in rapid succession.

As the four Twits try to protect themselves with arms held across their faces, another laughing, deep voice joins the chant.

"**TWITS, TWITS, TWITS!**" sing-songs Neville, cheerfully bashing his fists on his handlebars.

A whole blur of people now come running round the corner to see what's going on.

In among general kids and parents, I'm very glad to see the ones I recognize – Lulu, Granny Viv, and the rest of the staff and students of St Grizzle's – who are hurrying to our aid as if they somehow **mind-read** that one of our own was in trouble. Even Downboy is barking madly in support and Twinkle has just aimed her head at the bum of the tallest of Spencer's friends. He's screeching and running towards the safety of the nearby girls' loos.

At that moment, someone ELSE comes hurtling round the corner.

"Stop this! Stop it at once!" roars Mr Puddock. "Put those sponges down, girls – and stop making that dreadful racket, everyone! You too, Mr Scott!"

Neville looks sulkily at the head teacher as if he's a seven-year-old getting a telling-off instead of a seventy-something-year-old who's ancient enough to be Mr Puddock's father.

"This is OUTRAGEOUS behaviour," Mr Puddock continues, as the sponges are dumped and the chanting trails off. "Ms Murphy – I think you'd better take your students back to your OWN school straight away. I trust you'll deal with them appropriately."

"Yes, I will," says Lulu firmly. "Come on, everyone."

And so we begin to shuffle after our head teacher, passing Neville as we go.

"Peace and strength to you, little sista!" Neville says to Boo, who smiles shyly – and slaps a high five into the big hand he holds out to her.

It's at that same moment that a MUCH larger slap is heard in the dark-clouded sky above and all at once heavy rain tumbles like a giant bath's been upturned in the heavens.

As the storm hits, everyone in the playground runs to take cover under awnings and gazebos and rickety stalls.

Everyone except US.

"Let's go, St Grizelda's," Lulu calls out, holding her dripping head high and throwing her shoulders back in her soggy new T-shirt. We all do the same, while everyone else around us shudders and huddles in their makeshift shelters.

Without rushing, we troop out of the playground and out through the open gate, where Spencer's surprisingly nice mum waves us off from under a large golf umbrella, which she's sharing with her sticky baby.

"How silly to be afraid of a little bit of water," Lulu says, looking back through the railings at the cowed crowds of parents and children.

"It's like they think rain is DANGEROUS!" says one of the Newts.

"Or like it HURTS!" jokes another.

"Or like it's made of POISON that could turn you PURPLE and then KILL you!" Blossom chips in madly.

"OK, enough, enough," says Lulu, though when she turns to look over her shoulder I can see she's smiling. "Now, Newts, about throwing those sponges..."

The grinning Newts suddenly stop grinning. They look like half-drowned rats as the rain slaps their hair to their heads and runs in rivulets down their suddenly worried faces.

"Sorry..." they burble in overlapping unison.

The Newts say sorry a lot. Mainly because they're regularly caught doing things they probably shouldn't be doing.

"Oh, no," says Lulu, shaking her own sopping-wet head at Blossom and her classmates. "I WAS going to say ... **well done.**"

A Mexican wave of smiles ripples up and down our crocodile of kids.

"And Fungi Class – I'm SURE you can give me a fuller explanation of the incident than Mr Puddock was willing to hear."

"Oh, yes!" I burst out. "It all happened because—"

"Hold on, Dani," Lulu interrupts. "Before you tell me, I just need to remind everyone of Mr Puddock's advice to deal with you all APPROPRIATELY."

Lulu looks up and down the straggly line, her face unusually serious. Uh-oh.

"So when we get back to school," she adds after an uncomfortable pause, "I'm going to make you all hot chocolate with squirty cream and serve up ALL the cake you can eat. Is that punishment enough?"

"YAYYYYYYYY!"

Even Granny Viv, Miss Amethyst, Mademoiselle Fabienne and Toshio join in with the whoops and cheers.

Who knows what Mr Puddock and the huddling hordes in the playground must think of the happy racket they suddenly hear.

But who cares?

Like our lovely head teacher, we hold our heads high and stride off towards St Grizzle's. Lulu with her goat, girls and random boys trotting, jingling and zooming behind.

Who needs to be friends with Twits anyway...?

Chapter 5

Annoying Fnurrrpppps and Terrible Favours

A screen sort of mistake...

The rain is still sloshing down this evening, even heavier than it was in the afternoon.

Water trickles wiggly paths on the windowpanes, and gushes and gurgles down drainpipes. But we're all cosy and happy inside the sturdy stone walls of St Grizzle's.

Right now, it's nearly Newts-bedtime-o'clock, and they're cuddled and snuggled in their dorm with multiple new-but-old teddies from the fair, being read to by Boo. (Funny to think they're all the same age – Boo just seems older, smarter, and less *goblin*-ish, I suppose.)

The triplets, meanwhile, are holed up halfway down the staircase in their PJs, video-messaging their charity-worker parents before they go to bed. I hope their mum and dad have good hearing or great lip-reading skills – the mostly silent sisters were talking in their usual barely there whispers when I passed them earlier.

Downstairs, Angel and Klara are finishing

off a board game in the dining room with Mademoiselle Fabienne. Their fellow Conkers Yas and May-Belle have been watching an old movie in the school hall. It was about twins of divorced parents who swap places to fool their mum and dad, and Yas and May-Belle are hotly debating how exactly the twins' parents could've missed the switch.

Speaking of parents, Swan has come to join me and Arch on the beanbags at the back of the hall, while Zed is in Lulu's office, finishing a phone conversation with their dad in Hong Kong.

As Swan flops down on a spare beanbag, a small but very distinctive sound bursts out.

Fnurrrppp!

It's … well, there's no polite way of saying this – it's a *farting* sort of sound.

The hotly debating Yas and May-Belle glance round.

"NO! I'm NOT responsible for that!" Swan calls

out crossly to them.

Fnurrrppp!

"But where IS it coming from?" I wonder aloud, staring this way and that.

"Don't stress – it's me," Arch admits, wrangling his mobile out of his back pocket. "Well, technically, it's my new ringtone for calls from my dad."

"Your poor dad!" I say jokily, while expecting my buddy to answer his dad's call. He doesn't. Instead, Arch tosses the phone in the air and catches it like it's some toy.

Fnurrrppp!

"Poor Dad? Ha!" replies Arch, giving one of those not-funny-at-all kind of laughs. "You should hear the one I choose for calls from my mum. It's that '**UH-OH**' sound for wrong answers on quiz shows."

"Arch!" I snap, feeling less jokey all of a sudden.

"What?" he answers distractedly.

Throw.

Fnurrrppp!

Catch.

"You've GOT to talk to your parents!" I point out.

"Why should I?" he answers with a careless shrug.

"Cos they'll want to know how you're getting on here and they'll worry if you don't pick up," I tell him.

"Oh, they're WAY too busy fighting with each other to care about *me*," says Arch, flipping his phone as the farting sound farts on. "I mean, they both ask me the SAME questions ALL the time. They can't even be bothered to talk about me to each other."

Fnurrrppp!

"That's not true!" I say, frowning at my friend. "Just because they're having problems, doesn't mean they love you any less!"

"Whatever – I've decided to have a break from them both. So sorry, Dad – laterzzz..." Arch says to the phone with a sarky tone.

I picture nice Mr Kaminski at the other end of the phone. He's going through a sad break-up, is probably fretting madly about his son AND he's been reduced to a dumb fart noise on a phone.

Fnurrrppp!

You know, I totally love my best friend, but you can feel ALL different feelings at once about someone, can't you? At the moment I feel sorry for Arch and his difficult family situation, but I could cheerfully strangle him too for being so stubborn.

So when Granny Viv appears at the door of the hall and waves me over, I'm glad to get away from him and the **Fnurrrppp!**ing for a bit.

"Sorry to drag you off, Dani. It's just that I need a hand with something," says Granny Viv, as she heads towards the stairs. I notice she's holding a plastic bag under one arm.

"It's fine," I tell her as I follow her up the polished wooden steps. I'm just about to ask what she needs a hand with when Granny Viv starts up again.

"I know every second with a good friend is precious…"

"Mmm," I mumble in reply. It's very precious – unless your friend is being stubborn and annoying and **Fnurrrppp!**ing, like Arch is right now.

"Especially when it comes to Arch – I know how much you've missed him, Dani," Granny Viv continues, nodding and smiling at the whispery triplets as we pass them. "It's like me and Eric. Don't get me wrong, I LOVE being here with you but I do miss seeing him."

Eric is Granny Viv's best buddy, and he is an OAP.

Most people think that stands for Old Age Pensioner, but in Eric's case, it's Old Age Punk. He does gigs in pubs around my home town, singing shouty songs to not much of an audience.

"Mind you, Eric said he might pop up and visit me sometime this week," Granny Viv chats on as we reach the first-floor landing where the dorms are. But we're not stopping there, it seems – Granny Viv swivels around and begins to take the *next* set of stairs up to the staff quarters.

"He's at a bit of a loose end … had to cancel gigs this week as his car has to go in for an MOT, so he thought he might just hop on a couple of buses and come and check on me and Daisy!"

"Mmm," I mumble, as if I know what an MOT is.

I'm very happy for Granny Viv – it'll be nice for her to see her friend. But I do wish she'd get to the point. I *still* don't know what she wants me to help her with.

Then she gives me a clue.

"Here, hold that," she says, turning to hand me a hammer she's been hiding somewhere.

"Are we doing some late-night DIY?" I ask with a frown.

"Only a tiny bit, dear," says Granny Viv,

opening up the rustling plastic bag now we've arrived on the top floor. "I was clearing out an old cupboard under the stairs just now and it was quite the treasure trove! I came across a whole box of plastic red noses, a pile of crumpled old pink ballet tutus, lots of toy instruments and *these*."

From inside the bag, Granny Viv pulls a bundled string of dusty old fairy lights in the shape of flamingos.

I'm blinking hard at Granny Viv, trying to figure out what we're going to do. Smash them with the hammer?

"Anyway," Granny Viv carries on blithely, while trying to untangle the lights, "I thought that if we nail these fairy lights up around the door to Boo's dorm, it'll make it look very pretty. And less ... less..."

"Like a cupboard?" I suggest.

"Well, yes," Granny Viv says with a nod. "There is that."

Cos Boo DOES actually live in a cupboard. It says 'Linens' on the door in old-fashioned, gold-painted lettering, cos it's where servants in long-ago days used to keep the towels and things.

It's not as bad as it sounds – Boo chose the cupboard to be her very own, personal mini-dorm, since she wasn't at ALL keen on sharing. We've painted and decorated it, and the mattress fits in snugly. All the shelves are stacked with Boo's books, and draped in birdie bunting that Swan made specially, plus more fairy lights. There's even room for a guest... Up on the top shelf, beside a teeny window, is a plastic box specially filled with straw. Perfect for Boo's pet pigeon Marvin to hop into after a busy day's fluttering and cooing outside.

"So while Boo is busy reading to the Newts," says Granny Viv, handing me the tangly string of fairy lights, "I thought you could hold these in place and I'll tap a few pins in so—"

"Shh!" I shush my gran, and quickly point to the Linen-cupboard door.

It seems that Boo's already finished her

bedtime-story session with the Newts. And it seems she has company – I heard voices just now.

"Aw … is she talking to Marvin?" says Granny Viv, tuning into the sound of Boo's voice and stepping a little closer.

"NO!"

An angry little shout from inside makes us both jump.

"Well, I **LIKE** it. I like it **ALL**! And **DON'T** call him that nasty name. **GOODBYE**!"

"What on earth is going on in there?" Granny Viv whispers to me, before tapping on the door and calling out to Boo in a louder voice.

"Sweetheart…? Everything OK?"

There's no reply except for a sobbing sound, so Granny Viv quickly turns the brass handle and pulls open the door.

Boo is standing on her mattress, since there's no room for actual floor in there. Tears are streaming down her face. Marvin is perched behind her on his top shelf, his head bobbing in concern for his mistress.

"I made a mistake..." she snuffles miserably.

"What sort of mistake?" I ask.

"A *screen* sort of mistake..." says Boo, drooping like a deflating balloon on to the squashy duvet.

Me and Granny Viv shuffle in and squiggle ourselves down. There seem to be a lot more legs and elbows than you might expect.

"What do you mean, Boo?" asks Granny Viv, once she's settled, with her knees somewhere under her chin.

"My mum and dad were going to phone me tonight from Austria, before their concert. But today I saw Dani and everyone else doing *video calls* instead and I thought that looked kind of fun..."

Boo holds up the iPad.

"Aha..." mutters Granny Viv, running a hand through Boo's short and funky hair. "So your parents aren't fans of your new look, then?"

Boo shakes her head.

"They're *very* cross that I cut off all my hair," says Boo, tears pooling in her pale grey eyes. "But it's not just that... I gave them a guided tour of my room and that made them cross as well."

"Hmm... Maybe it would've been better if your mum and dad HEARD rather than SAW you," I say, thinking how unimpressed snooty Mr and

71

Mrs Featherton-Snipe would have been with their newly shorn daughter and her live-in cupboard, especially since they're paying for the privilege.

"Technology," Granny Viv sighs, tapping the iPad with her index finger. "It's got a lot to answer for, if you ask me. It can cause such a lot of trouble."

"Yes, but it *can* be brilliant, too," I say in defence of technology, and thinking how amazing it was to see my thousands-of-miles-away mum this morning. "And remember, you can do cool stuff with it, like make mini-movies. Boo's been getting into that – haven't you, Boo? Hey, maybe you could teach Granny Viv how to make a little film! Wouldn't that be fun?"

Granny Viv seemed to spot that I was trying to distract the snuffly girl hunkered between us. So she joined in straight away, saying, "Oh, yes please, Boo! And then I could send films to my friend Eric, showing him funny things like the outfits the statue of St Grizzle's turns up wearing every day..."

Sadly, the distracting failed dismally.

"And then... And then they saw Marvin!" says Boo, hiccupping with hurt feelings and not hearing a word we'd just said. "And my dad said 'Boudicca, there is VERMIN in that horrible cupboard with you', and that made ME very cross cos Marvin is nice and not at all vermin-y, and I said so and that I love my room and it's not horrible and then I told them that actually I don't want to be called Boudicca any more thank you and please call me Boo like everyone at school does, and they got even *crosser* and their crossness has just made me feel all

AAARGGHH!"

That last sentence comes out in one breathless, breathtaking whoosh, and is quite the most words me and Granny Viv have heard Boo use all at once. We're both so stunned that we don't notice straight away that we have company.

POP!

"Well, you're ALL going to feel pretty AAARGGHH! in a second when I tell you about the phone call Lulu just took," says Swan, leaning on the doorframe and expertly wrapping gum around her finger.

"What – have Boo's parents called to complain *already*?" I ask, doing some quick mental maths and figuring it's only been a couple of minutes since Boo's disastrous video-chat ended. Surely that doesn't give enough time for...

- Mr and Mrs Featherton-Snipe to phone Lulu
- rant at her
- the call to end, and
- Swan to run up here to tell us all about it. Does it?

"Oh, I think Lulu would have preferred to take a HUNDRED moany phone calls from grumpy

74

parents rather than THIS one..." Swan drawls.

"Don't keep us in suspense, Swan, dear," Granny Viv urges her. "Who called?"

"Mr Puddock!" Swan announces.

"Huh? Why's the head teacher of the Twits calling Lulu on a Sunday evening?" I ask. "Was it to do with the Newts chucking sponges at Spencer and his friends?"

"Nope. Mr Puddock asked for a favour," says Swan. "A really, really **terrible** favour..."

Along with everyone else squashed in the cupboard, I hold my breath, dreading what that really, really terrible favour could be...

Chapter 6
Preparing for the Pesky Guests

And the wrong clothes...

It's nine a.m. on Monday morning, and the sky is grey and grumpy with clouds – but at least it's finally stopped raining.

So far we have done normal Monday morning things, which at St Grizzle's don't tend to be very normal.

First, we were woken up by Lulu singing her cheerful 'Good morning, good MORNING!' song on the tannoy that runs through every dorm and room in the school. (Though today she didn't sound *quite* as cheerful as usual, with good reason.)

Then we had pyjama assembly – with breakfast – which happens every Monday, because ... well, same as everything at St Grizzle's, why not?

It was at assembly that Lulu told the whole school about the really, really **terrible** favour she's been asked to do.

"I still think our mum should have said *no* to

Mr Puddock," grumbles Swan, frowning off towards the school gates while shoving her fists deep into the pockets of her cut-off dungarees.

The whole school's here, hovering by the statue of St Grizzle to welcome our soon-to-arrive 'guests'. Well, the whole school, except for Lulu, for some reason. And actually, there are *even* more people missing from our impatiently waiting line ... I mean the Newts have disappeared up the nearest tree and Boo is swaying on the rope swing with Marvin on her shoulder, teaching the entranced triplets to coo just like him. Meanwhile, the Conkers are sitting on the front steps of the school, huddled around someone's tablet and giggling at a Japanese animation Toshio found for them.

As for Toshio, he's currently trying to hold on to both Downboy and Twinkle's leads, while being dragged into the flower beds where Twinkle has just spotted a snack-ish looking rose bush.

Even Granny Viv has wandered off, holding up her phone in search of a signal by the look of it.

So the only people actually standing in (a loose) line are *my* class, Mademoiselle Fabienne and Miss Amethyst.

"But Swan – your maman had no choice about the favour, did she?" says Mademoiselle Fabienne, who suddenly produces a flouncy umbrella, just in case the rain starts again and makes the dainty fabric flowers of her hair garland go saggy and soggy.

"Mademoiselle Fabienne is right," Miss Amethyst agrees. "With the flooding at Twittering School, Lulu could hardly say no to helping out."

Yesterday's storm had stormed and the rain had rained ... until the normally chirpy river at the bottom of the village school's playground burst its banks and went barging and slooshing into the new extension. Corridors turned into streams, classroom floors turned into ponds and the fancy main hall was a mud-coloured lake.

"Exactly!" says Lulu, coming to join us at last. "Naturally, I said we were happy to help out! I'm sure Mr Puddock would've done the same if it were the other way around."

"I bet he wouldn't," Swan growls in reply to her mother. "Anyway, what took you so long?"

"I was talking a call from Boo's parents," says Lulu, rubbing her right ear. "And I'm still a bit deaf from all the shouting…"

Lulu might be making a joke about what was probably a pretty awful conversation, but none of us are listening. Instead we're all staring. Cos something isn't right with Lulu.

Her hair, for a start – it's all … well, brushed and shiny.

And her clothes are wrong. A skirt? A shirt? Some smart-ish shoes? Where are her shorts? A cute logo T-shirt? Her flip-flops?

"What ARE you wearing?" Swan demands.

"Just... Just something I found in the back of my wardrobe," says Lulu, sounding ever-so-slightly sheepish. "Hey, NEWTS – come down out of that tree now! You'd better not be dirty after I asked you to wash your hands and faces properly!"

There's a rinkling and a tinkling and then a bunch of surprised faces peer out of leafy branches.

The rest of us stare with startled gazes, too.

Lulu's usually the one who's happy to teach for the entire day with look-alike tribal stripes of mud across her nose, smeared there by some Newt during a nature walk in the woods. And I swear she had glitter in her eyebrows for THREE WHOLE DAYS last week.

"Oh, girls... I know they're lovely, but I did ask you NOT to wear the bells today," Lulu adds wearily. "Could you come down and take them off, please? Quickly, before our visitors get—"

"Hey, places, everyone!" we hear Granny Viv call out, putting her phone away and hurrying back to our welcome line. "The Twits are here!"

The nearby Conkers, triplets and Boo jump to it, sending Marvin hurtling into the air, till he lands on top of a strangely *non*-decorated St Grizzle, I suddenly notice.

Using superhuman strength, Toshio drags a stubborn Twinkle and a lolloping Downboy over to the line, too. (Why ARE they on leads today, when they're usually allowed to lollop freely?)

The Newts don't come out of the tree as if they can sense that something is off-kilter in our corner of the world today.

"Hello, there!" Lulu calls out and waves to Mr Puddock, who – along with a younger man – leads a class of kids dressed identically in green sweatshirts and black trousers.

Mr Puddock doesn't wave back.

The younger man does, and smiles, too, till he gets a sharp sideways glance of disapproval and lowers his hand.

"Hey, isn't that—"

"The guy who was on the **Guess How Many Marbles Are in the Jar** stall yesterday!" Arch finishes Zed's sentence for him.

Yes, of course I recognize him now. He was the nice man who amazingly *didn't* get ratty when runaway Twinkle knocked the whole table over. And now I think about it, I've seen him even before that, around the village with a bunch of Twits – he's Spencer's teacher.

"There are SO many of them!" says Boo, quickly shuffling closer to Arch and me as she stares wide-eyed and wary at the incomers drifting towards us.

"There're twenty-eight. Lulu said that's how many is in this Year 6 class," I tell her.

"More than the whole of our school," mutters Swan, with a defiant ***POP!*** of bubblegum.

I guess it could have been worse. Only *part* of Twittering school was flooded … the part nearest the river. According to Lulu the Year 4s and 5s were moving to the gym in the older section of the school for a few days, while giant heaters dry out the mess in the new extension.

But there was nowhere for the Year 6s to go ...
till Mr Puddock decided to call Lulu. It must have
choked him to do that. (Granny Viv reckons he
only did it cos he'd figured a school as big as ours
would have a traditional big hall and stage, and
wanted it for the Year 6 show.)

"Lovely to see you all! Come this way!" Lulu
sing-songs, waving everyone to follow her inside.

"Good day to you, Ms Murphy," Mr Puddock
replies dryly, without a hint of cheerfulness in
his voice.

Bringing up the rear of the line of Twits is
Spencer and his mates, I notice – all equally
cheerless.

The *rest* of the Twits, meanwhile, are gawping
around – at the school, at us, at the bug-eyed
wildlings' faces peering out of a strangely tinkling
tree at them. One girl Twit gives a little scream
of shock till Mr Puddock sternly shushes her.

They gawp even more when Toshio gives

86

every one of them a polite bow as they pass.
A few Twits smile back, or at least try a friendly
pat of our pets. (Downboy slobbers on them in
return, while Twinkle attempts to nibble the cuffs
of their sweatshirts.)

"There are an *awful* lot of boys," says Boo,
tugging at my arm as we turn to traipse after
Lulu. "I don't really want any more. They might
be silly."

"Oh, but silly is good. We *like* silly at St
Grizzle's, Boo!" I remind her.

"I meant BAD silly," whispers Boo. "Like the
boy with the big floofy hair and his friends."

"One of that group IS a girl," I say, feeling
I should point that fact out.

"Well, she's as BAD silly as they are," Boo
mutters, holding on tight to the back of Arch's
T-shirt. (I can see that her tugging is pulling at
the collar and is ever-so-slightly choking him, but
Arch is too kind to say.)

As we shuffle into the cool, wood-panelled, tiled-floor entrance hall I glance back and check out Spencer and his buddies – and see them pointing and snickering at lovely Toshio and mimicking his equally lovely welcoming bow.

How absolutely DARE they!

Honestly, these pesky guests have only been here thirty seconds but it's already been WAY too long.

I feel like stomping right on over to them and telling them they're a bunch of nasty, horrible...

"Come on! Let's all go in the hall, lovely people!" Miss Amethyst calls out, interrupting my **grrrrs**.

With a flap of her arms, she tries to shoo everyone along the corridor. It's tricky, though, cos lots of Twits have stalled, **"oohing"** and **"ahhing"** and pointing at the elegant sweeping staircase that's like something out of a movie set. Others are causing a traffic jam by staring at the

framed staff photos on the wall. There are

only five, and about twenty spaces where

other teachers' photos *used* to hang till the

original staff all packed their bags and

scarpered.

There's even MORE **"oohing"** and

"ahhing" from the Twits as we finally all

make it into the hall.

"No, no, no, Twittering Year 6. Sit on

the FLOOR, down at the FRONT,

please!" Mr Puddock orders, stopping his

squealing students in their tracks as they

rush for our colourful beanbags and giant

floor cushions.

"Awww…" they grumble, but do what they're

told, settling their black-trousered bottoms on

polished hard wood.

Which leaves everyone from St Grizzle's to

rustle into the luxury of our squidgy seats at the

back. Including the Newts, who are now sneaking

in like jingle-jangling ninja-goblins.

"A warm welcome to St Grizelda's! How FANTASTIC to meet you all!" Lulu calls out over the sound of shuffling, chit-chat and hubbubbing. She gives a little laugh, every bit as jingly as the Newts' Afghani bells and baubles.

"Don't you think Lulu sounds a bit nervous?" I whisper to Granny Viv, who's settled down beside me.

"You know, I suspect she might be worried about Mr Puddock's reaction to the school," Granny Viv whispers back.

"Really?" I hiss. "You think she's nervous of HIM?"

"Mmm, unfortunately, I think so. She's tidied things up too much, including herself. When I was out filming in the grounds earlier—"

"You were filming?" I interrupt, realizing THAT'S what Granny Viv was doing while we were waiting for the Twits to arrive. I thought she was maybe trying to contact Eric about his possible visit.

"Yes, I was filming. Remember, you suggested to Boo that she gives me some lessons in making mini-movies and whatnot?" Granny Viv whispers.

"Well, yeah, but I didn't think she was paying any attention," I mumble back.

"She was just a bit upset at the time, but she's certainly keen and ended up giving me a lesson before breakfast AND some homework," Granny Viv whispers some more. "Anyway, AS I was saying, when I was filming in the grounds earlier, I caught Lulu doing something totally out of character. She was taking a very nice apron and knitted beanie OFF the statue!"

Granny Viv **tsks**, as if this is very unnatural behaviour. Which it really is.

I want to ask her why someone as fun and free-spirited as Lulu would care about what someone as dull and uptight as Mr Puddock thinks, but a surprising noise twangs above the chit-chattering and hubbubbing in the hall. Spotting that Lulu was struggling to get the attention of the hyper-excited guests, Mademoiselle Fabienne has picked up her guitar and strummed a few calming chords. The unexpected sound – and the sight of a lady who's dressed a little bit like a grown-up fairy – startles the visiting Twits SO much that they instantly shut up and stare at her open-mouthed. Someone ELSE staring open-mouthed at Mademoiselle Fabienne is the Year 6 teacher. He's blinking at her as if he has never seen anyone so bonkers.

Or beautiful. Or both.

As for Mr Puddock … he's looking at our art teacher as if he'd like to give her detention for not wearing the appropriate school uniform.

"Thank you, mademoiselle," says Lulu, clapping her appreciation. "Well, as I was saying, welcome, staff and students of Twittering. We at St Grizelda's are VERY pleased indeed to be able to help you out in your hour of need. And please feel free to stay as long as you like!"

"No, no, no – we'll only be here for two or three days, Ms Murphy," Mr Puddock says swiftly, walking up to Lulu's side. "That'll be *quite* enough."

"Um, fine," says Lulu, slightly taken aback at the gruffness of Mr Puddock's tone, though she brightens her smile as she turns to face the Twits directly in front of her. "Now, then, Year 6 – I've heard from Mr Puddock how hard you've all been working on your show, so we're very happy to offer you our stage and hall. Which means your performance for the residents of the Huddleton Retirement Lodge can go ahead tomorrow night as planned!"

A few "hurray!"s break out from some grateful Twits, but Mr Puddock quickly silences their appreciation with a slicing action of one hand.

"Well, uh, time for some quick introductions," says Lulu, trying to keep the mood perky. "So I'm Lulu, and I'm the head teacher here..."

Cue lots of mutterings of surprise at the idea of calling a head teacher by their first name.

Cue another silencing hand slice from Mr Puddock.

Lulu gives him a puzzled frown before carrying on.

"...and we have our teachers Miss Amethyst and Mademoiselle Fabienne..."

Miss Amethyst gives a gracious, queenly wave of her hand, while Mademoiselle Fabienne shyly wiggles her fingers and blushes. A few Twits wave and wiggle back, I'm pleased to see.

"...and if you have any questions or need directions, Reception's where you need to go, and Toshio is who you need to speak to!"

Lulu points to Toshio, who's standing at the very back of the hall, holding the leads of both Twinkle and Downboy in one hand. He's nodding his head in time to some pop track he's clearly listening to on his giant white headphones. Realizing he's being talked about, Toshio drops the headphones down around his neck, then smiles and bows quickly. Snorts ring out from a bunch of Twits – I turn my head sharply and am not at all shocked to see the snorters are Spencer and his friends.

"And finally," says Lulu, "there's our cook and general wonder woman, Granny Viv!"

On the beanbag next to me, Granny Viv suddenly leaps up and strikes a dramatic, superhero pose, and a ripple of titters runs around the room. Mr Puddock, however, looks deeply unimpressed at the sight of a grandmother goofing around and scowls at her as if she's a naughty kid disrupting a lesson. Looks like he's as impressed by Granny Viv as he is with Mademoiselle Fabienne – which is not at all.

"Do you think he's about to send me to the naughty step?" Granny Viv mutters to me as she settles back into the beanbag.

He might be. He's about to speak for sure, but Lulu spots that and gets in first.

"So you've met the staff, and you'll get to know the pupils in no time," she says, swooping an arm out towards us all at the back. "And I'm sure you'll enjoy the lessons here at St Grizelda's. In fact, the first one of the day is our very popular circus skills class!"

Enthusiastic **"ooo-OOO-ooh"**s fan out across the Year 6 class – till Mr Puddock practically pushes Lulu aside with a bunch of now wildly slicing hand movements and takes over.

"Thank you, *Ms Murphy*, but we WON'T be taking you up on your **kind** offer," he announces briskly, making the word '**kind**' sound like '**rubbish**'.

A long, disappointed group sigh rumbles in the front rows. Mr Puddock squashes it quiet with a narrow-eyed stare.

"Here's what's happening – Mr Nayar, our Year 6 teacher, will look after our pupils' education in the mornings while I'm at the main school in the village, overseeing lessons and the flood clean-up," Mr Puddock says curtly, like some scarily bossy sergeant-major. "Then in the afternoons, I will come back here and take charge of rehearsals for the show. So we'll need to commandeer a spare classroom, **Ms Murphy** – and I know you have LOTS of empty classrooms these days."

"Right... Well, we'll see what we can sort out

for you, Mr Puddock," Lulu says in a calm, measured voice, which makes me very proud of her. After all, her fellow head teacher has just tossed aside her goodwill like a crumpled, snotty hankie.

I glance around at Swan and Zed and the rest of the St Grizzle's gang. This is *awful*. Mr Puddock is being rude and ungrateful and unkind, and Lulu – who is always generous and thoughtful and sweet – doesn't deserve that.

Fnurrrppp!

The farty sound echoes around the hall.

I glance round at my best buddy, but his head is down as he frantically pats his jeans back and front, trying to locate his phone so he can turn the volume down. At last he finds it but can't seem to wrestle it out of the stiff denim pocket.

Fnurrrppp!

That dumb alert – it might have bugged me yesterday, but this morning I'm glad to hear it, cos it suddenly bursts the bubble of awkwardness in the big room.

The Newts start tee-heeing first, then the triplets of Otter class cover their faces as they giggle, then the Conkers start full-on sniggering.

It's infectious, spreading to the Twits like the best virus ever.

Within seconds, EVERYONE is laughing out loud.

Fnurrrppp!

"Stop it! SILENCE!" orders Mr Puddock, but it's too late – he's being swamped by a tidal wave of silliness.

"This is GOOD silly, isn't it?" asks serious-as-ever Boo, gazing up at me to check if she should be joining in.

"It's the BEST kind," I tell her, and am rewarded with a shy smile.

A small smattering of hope fizzles in my tummy.

Maybe our guests won't be as pesky as we first thought. (Most of them anyway.)

Same as there's good silly and bad silly, it looks like there might be plenty of good Twits as well as bad Twits. A LOT more, in fact.

So maybe – just maybe – the next few days will turn out to be EXCELLENT fun!

But just to be sure, I'll keep my fingers as tightly crossed as I can without cutting off the blood supply...

Chapter 7
Clowning Around

And snuffly
red noses...

"MEHHHH!" Twinkle protests, yanking at the long rope she's been tethered with. Some leggings hanging on the washing line are *cruelly* out of gnashing range.

Downboy's tied to a long leash of rope, too, which is making him so fed up he's flopped sulkily on the grass like an unhappy furry rug.

I'd go over and give them both a cuddle, but circus skills class is about to start, AND we're getting an unexpected pep talk from Lulu.

"So can you please, PLEASE promise me you'll all be on your best behaviour for the next few days?" says our head teacher, gazing beseechingly around the semicircle of girls and random boys gathered on the back lawn.

"We promise," everyone mumbles half-heartedly back at her.

"Excuse me, Lulu, dear," Granny Viv interrupts, putting her hand in the air. "It doesn't seem as if Mr Puddock is on HIS best behaviour, so why should WE be?"

It's a cheeky but reasonable question. All eyes swivel towards Lulu, who looks a little embarrassed – and a little desperate.

"I just don't want him thinking badly of us OR telling people that we're not a good school."

"But you know we are!" Zed protests.

"Yes, of course I do," Lulu answers with a that's-obvious shrug.

"So why do you care what HE thinks?" Swan demands of her mum.

"Well, the thing is, Mr Puddock is the spokesperson of the head teachers' association for the area. He also knows lots of important people at the local council and newspaper. If it *wrongly* got out that St Grizelda's wasn't a good school, then fewer and fewer students might choose to come here," Lulu says slowly, picking her words carefully. "And if THAT were to happen, it would get a bit ... tricky."

"No, it wouldn't! There'd be LOTS more SPACE for all of us!" Blossom yells out.

Blossom's too young, I guess, to figure out what Lulu is trying to say. But I'm not. And with a twist in my tummy I realize Lulu's saying St Grizzle's might eventually close if there aren't enough students to keep it open...

"Anyway, I'm going to leave you to do your circus skills with Granny Viv today as I have a conversation to continue," Lulu concludes, smiling at everyone as she walks away.

A conversation with Boo's disgruntled parents, I bet...

As soon as Lulu disappears through the back door, Granny Viv pulls a box and a big bag out from under the nearby picnic table. She has a twinkle in her eye and a minxy, red-lipped smile on her face.

"How about looking like *proper* circus performers today?" she suggests, thunking the box of red noses on the table and shaking out the tumble of crumpled pink ballet tutus beside it. There're some dusty palettes of face paint in the muddled pile, too. "Let's show those Twits what the best-ever PE lesson looks like, eh?"

And for the next hour, that's exactly what we do.

Dressed up and gee'd up, we tumble and juggle, we unicycle and trapeze across the grass, while the Year 6 Twits sit inside a classroom, staring wistfully out at us as they plod along with their regular lessons in whatever. Even Mr Nayar looks like he wishes he could join in and come and try out the stilts. Or perhaps he's staring at Mademoiselle Fabienne... Inspired by our spectacular circus makeover today she's not only used her artistic talent (and the face paints) to clown-ify us, but also accompanied our **whirling** and **wheeing** with jolly, stomping waltzy tunes strummed with gusto on her guitar.

Actually, ONE person hasn't been watching us wistfully. Spencer and his blond quiff are easy to spot, of course, and that sneer of his ... it's so obvious, so snidey, even from a distance. You can probably see it from the moon.

But we're all having too good a time to care about Sneery McSneerface. In fact, we're having SUCH a good time that we don't bother to get changed for our next, normal lesson (science with Miss Amethyst).

And we don't bother to get changed for lunch either.

"GOT to show this to Eric – he'll love it!" says Granny Viv, filming one long dining-room table stuffed with all four St Grizzle's classes.

Granny Viv reckons it's kind of punk to look the way we look, when the children sitting at the other long dining-room table are in typical, totally matching uniform.

As for me, I think our goofy get-ups might help

break the ice with the Twits, or at least the nice ones.

"Some of them are smiling over at us," I point out to Swan, Zed and Arch.

"Yeah, but lots of them are whispering and staring at us like we're freaks," mutters Swan.

"I suppose..." I reluctantly agree.

"It's as if they've never seen twenty-two people eating pudding in red noses, tutus and full clown make-up," jokes Arch, who's wearing all that AND his back-to-front baseball cap.

At least Mr Nayar has appreciated our style.

"Well, I've never had a lunch like THIS before!" I hear him say from the nearby table where the staff are sitting.

Luckily for us, Mr Puddock isn't back yet from overseeing the rescue work back at the village school. Unluckily, he'll be back after lunch to supervise the rehearsals for the show.

"I'm glad to hear that!" says Lulu, smiling at the

Twits' Year 6 teacher.

"Yes, but are you talking about the clown gang or the fabulous food, Mr Nayar?" Miss Amethyst asks, before cheekily adding, "Or perhaps it's the view...?"

Mr Nayar blushes and helps himself to another mouthful of Granny Viv's excellent toffee-cake pudding, and pretends he doesn't notice that an equally flustered Mademoiselle Fabienne is sitting directly opposite him...

A nudge in the ribs with a sharp elbow drags my attention away from the possible twinkles of romance at the next table.

"What?" I ask, turning to Arch.

"Boo's a bit upset," he says, leaning back so I can see the sad little clown sitting on the other side of him.

Uh-oh – matching trickles of tears are washing clear trails down her white clown make-up. Her nose is probably red from crying too, under the plastic clown nose she's wearing.

"What's wrong, Boo?" I ask, leaning across Arch to talk to his sorrowful shadow.

Snuffling, she holds up her mobile so I can see the message from her dad that must've just pinged through.

> Boudicca – despite lengthy discussions with and assurances from your head teacher, your mother and I have concluded that St Grizelda's might not be a suitable school for you. Therefore we're currently reviewing the situation. We'll try you again later.

Gulp.

"I'm a hundred per cent sure Lulu WILL convince your parents to let you stay, Boo," I try to reassure her. "She'll keep talking to them. She'll wear them down, you'll see!"

Truthfully? I'm a hundred per cent sure I'm not sure about that at all. I mean, now that I think about Boo's video-chat last night, from Mr and

Mrs Featherton-Snipe's point of view it must've looked bizarre. Boo's shorn hair, the cell-shaped cupboard draped in fairy lights and bunting, the pet rat-with-wings (bet THAT's how her parents see Marvin) ... it must've seemed like their daughter was being held hostage by mad Christmas elves or something.

"Yeah, like Dani says, Lulu will sort it out," agrees Arch, putting a protective arm round his mini-me. "In the meantime, Boo, I'm going to make sure you have a ton of fun. OK?"

"OK!" Boo gazes up and smiles a watery smile.

Aw ... isn't Arch lovely?

"And like we talked about," Arch continues, "just carry on ignoring your parents if they're upsetting you. In fact, give me your phone and I'll add those ringtones..."

Huh...?

I'm about to tell Arch I'm not sure I think much of his dodgy-sounding advice when the dining room is suddenly filled with an ear-splitting

CLANG! CLANG! CLANG! CLANG!

Granny Viv has swapped filming for attention-grabbing, and the whole roomful of Twits and clowns sits bolt upright at the racket of her metal tray cymbals.

"Right, everyone!" she calls out. "We all take turns helping out here. So can I have some volunteers to bring the plates and cutlery through to the kitchen, please?"

She smiles when she sees a sea of hands rise

112

up in the air, including lots of willing Twits' hands.

Then I frown as I see the four Twits at the end of the table slink out of their seats, like they're aiming to sneak out of the dining-room door without being seen.

But before they vanish, Spencer pauses – and for a second I think he's maybe thought better of their escape plans. That's till I see him very deliberately flick his fingers at a close by tumbler of squash, which goes spinning, spiralling and spilling all over the table and on to the floor...

When everyone turns to see where the sharp, plastic **thunk** came from, Spencer and his sniggering crew are nowhere to be seen.

You know, if we didn't have to help clear up, I'd be tempted to sneak after them. I can't imagine they're just going to quietly wander around the school, commenting on how nice it is... Just what might they get up to, I wonder?

"Oh dear, looks like there's been a bit of a spill

over there," Granny Viv booms, distracting me. "Never mind, we can get it mopped up. And, hey – if everyone helps get this place tidied quickly, we might have time to play around with the circus equipment before Mr Puddock gets back!"

As delighted cheers break out from the Twits – and even Mr Nayar – Swan sidles up beside me.

"Pity my mum doesn't teach magic tricks instead of circus skills," she says, as she expertly scoops up piles of dirty plates. "Cos then we could make Spencer and his mates disappear in a puff of smoke."

"Or –" I begin, coming up with a MUCH better idea – "we could just cut Spencer in half!"

You know, I suddenly feel inspired to make a mini-movie, perhaps involving a chopping board and a carrot as a main actor...

Chapter 8
Roll Up, Roll Up, for the Worst Show in Town

And DON'T sing along...

"I'm WAITING...!" Mr Puddock growls into a microphone.

He's up on the stage, expecting total silence.

It's not going to happen.

First, cos there's still some tinkling going on among the Newts, even though Lulu made them take off and hand in their bells and baubles ahead of this afternoon's performance.

Second, cos Granny Viv decided that if we *have* to sit through the rehearsal of the Twits' show, then we need popcorn, and lots of it.

Apart from the occasional jingle-jangle, the rustling and nom-nom-ing, there's another couple of noises disturbing the peace. Downboy is asleep and snoring somewhere under the stage after slipping his long lead and doing a runner sometime during lunch. Twinkle, meanwhile, is still tied up and can be heard "MEH!"ing at the top of her goaty lungs out in the garden.

"CAN IT JUST START, PLEASE?" Blossom bellows at Mr Puddock, and her fellow Newts join in with a few "YAY!"s of agreement.

Gasps and giggles break out among the beanbag-seated audience, the Twits obviously taken aback by Blossom's bluntness. Boo and Granny Viv are right in front of me – Boo's helping Granny Viv film the show – and their little and larger shoulders are shaking. But it's not *just* the audience – giggles are erupting behind the scenes, too. In fact, I see quite a few grinning faces peeking out of the curtains on either side of the stage.

Mr Puddock is not grinning. Mr Puddock is scowling so much he might give himself a migraine. Mr Puddock forgets to lower the microphone he's holding and mutters, "Shower of gremlins..." for all to hear.

"Shush, girls!" Lulu says, rustling herself around on her own beanbag to tell off Blossom and the Newts. "Remember your manners!"

"She'd be better off saying that to Mr Puddock," says Swan, forgetting to lower her own voice. Except I don't think she DID forget.

"AND Spencer and his friends," I mumble back.

"Right!" Mr Puddock starts again, through gritted teeth. "AS I was saying, this show is entitled **'Keep Calm and Carry On'**..."

Sounds like it should be his motto for this week, I think to myself.

"...which is a slogan from the Second World War," Mr Puddock continues. "I wrote and devised the show with the old folks at the retirement home in mind. They may be frail and feeble now, but this should be a wonderful wander down memory lane for them!"

I frown a little at Mr Puddock's words. I mean, of course I don't know the other residents at the Huddleton Retirement Lodge, but I certainly don't think Neville, the man we met at the fair yesterday, could be described as 'frail' or 'feeble'. From what I saw of him, I think Neville might rev up his motorized scooter and run over the toes of anyone who *dared* call him that.

And if someone like Mr Puddock ever called Granny Viv's friend Eric 'old', he'd probably find himself serenaded at close range with the loudest, rudest punk song Eric could think of...

"So," Mr Puddock booms loudly, "will you please put your hands together for—"

PLINKY-PLONKY-PLINKY-PLONKY an old-fashioned tune starts up from the side of the stage.

"Sorry, sir!" Mr Nayar calls out, looking down in a panic at the laptop in front of him, which

Angel rigged up to the sound system. "Started that too early!"

Mr Puddock gives his teacher a death-ray stare, before finishing his introduction.

"Put your hands together, St Grizelda's, for **'Keep Calm and Carry On'!**"

As the plinky-plonky intro music starts up again, we wait to be entertained.

Sadly, there's nothing very entertaining about what comes next.

The Year 6 Twits drone song after song after song, all of them dirgy and dull.

They sing about packing things in a kitbag.

They sing about a few birds flying over some cliffs in Dover.

They sing about a funny-sounding place called Tipperary and how it's a long way away.

They even sing about rabbits run, run, running.

"These are actually quite catchy songs," Granny Viv turns round and says to me over her shoulder at one point. "How can they make them sound so awful?"

It's not just the singing that's awful, the acting is, too. Well, if you can call lots of endless marching (the boy Twits) and hankie-waving (the girl Twits) acting. And Spencer spent all HIS time manoeuvring his way to the front, using his elbows and dirty looks to get there.

"Keep Calm and Nod Off," whispers Arch, as he nudges the beanbag in front, where a Newt has curled up and started zzzz-ing.

After what feels like an eternity, the music finally stops, and the Year 6s stand on the stage, self-consciously saluting.

Because we're nice, we all manage a smattering of applause.

"Bravo! Bravo!" Mr Puddock calls out to his performers. "Great work, Year 6! And I'll bring the costumes tomorrow, so that you'll really feel the part for the dress rehearsal. Now if we can quickly file offstage and—"

"EXCUSE ME!" Blossom shouts out, waving a tinkling hand in the air. "MR PUDDLE, can I ask a QUESTION, PLEASE?"

"Er, yes, what is it?" Mr Puddock turns and says impatiently.

"WHY are all those songs so BORING?"

"Oof," Arch mutters beside me. All around there's the sound of rustling as people wince in their beanbags. The students on stage all gawp open-mouthed and let their salutes droop.

"These songs are not 'boring', little girl!" he snaps. "They are rousing anthems that kept up the spirits of everyone during the Second World

122

War," Mr Puddock splutters on. "They are still great favourites of soldiers and servicemen, even today. And frankly, I'm surprised you haven't been taught that at school. Or perhaps I'm NOT that surprised..."

There's a sudden rustle as Lulu pushes herself upright and readies herself to respond. However Blossom isn't finished.

"But MY DADDY is a soldier and HE wouldn't like this stuff," she announces matter-of-factly. "HE likes RIHANNA!"

For the second time that day, Mr Puddock is suddenly like a lone granite island in a bouncy ocean of laughter. Even Mr Nayar is hunched down behind the laptop, his shoulders heaving.

If looks could kill, I think the whole of St Grizelda's and very probably the Year 6 Twits, too, would be stone dead right now...

Chapter 9
'Accidents' Happen

And the scribbled somethings...

"Nice songs! Thank you very much! Bye bye!" Toshio calls out from the reception window.

The white band of his headphones has tilted forward, so it looks from the front as if he's wearing a plastic halo.

He waves and smiles at the Year 6s and Mr Nayar as they leave, and they smile and wave back. All except for one small group...

"Ni' song! Thang you velly much!" a mean, mimicking voice calls out, then Spencer and his sniggering friends tumble out of the open double doors and down the front steps.

"Did you hear that?" says Zed, sounding shocked.

"Yep," I answer at the same time as Swan and Arch.

I wonder if they're wishing – same as I am right now – that there was a pit of piranhas at the bottom of the front steps for Spencer to fall into.

Luckily, I don't think Toshio caught any of that nasty impression. He's just put his headphones back over his ears as he heads out of the office and into the emptying entrance hall.

"Goodbye, *Ms Murphy*," says Mr Puddock in an icy tone, gliding by our head teacher without glancing her way.

His face is as stern and grey as his suit. He's not only furious at losing control at the welcoming assembly and the performance this afternoon, he's also furious with Granny Viv for the 'Health and Safety violations' he came across when he turned up at school after lunch. In other words, he's cross that lots of Year 6 Twits were having a ball with the juggling, tumbling and general circus-ing.

"Bye! See you tomorrow, Year 6!" Lulu calls out cheerfully over Mr Puddock's shoulder, as she stands in the doorway to watch the Twits being marched off down the driveway.

Over Lulu's shoulder I spot Marvin outside, fluttering sharply away from his perch on the head of St Grizzle. And did I hear the tiny plink of a piece of gravel thunking off the statue? And could that piece of gravel have been thrown by Spencer, by any chance, since he's bent over laughing and pointing out the startled pigeon to his friends?

I wouldn't expect anything less from Spencer. I mean, from what I know of him so far, he's not the type to stick to just sneers. I bet he's got plenty of nasty little tricks up his sweatshirt sleeves for us over the next couple of days.

"Right, time to relax…" says Lulu, as she turns

and closes the heavy doors behind her. Immediately, her shoulders sag with relief and she kicks off her stiff shoes like she's kicking off the whole uncomfortable day.

The rest of St Grizzle's are already chilling out. Miss Amethyst and Mademoiselle Fabienne are sitting in the garden with a calming pot of peppermint tea. The triplets have persuaded Boo to go into the woods and teach them more bird trills. Angel and Yas have gone to set a still tied-up Twinkle free, while Klara is cartwheeling across the lawn. May-Belle said she was going to de-stress by listening to gloomy Goth music on her bed, and all ten Newt clowns were last seen with a stolen packet of Hobnobs, running off to the tree house.

And that leaves four Fungi lurking here in the entrance hall with Lulu.

"Flip-flops?" offers Swan, holding her mum's favourite pair out to her.

"Thank you, darling – that's very thoughtful," says Lulu, quickly slipping them on. "So how was today for you guys?"

"Torture," Swan says flatly, then blows and **POP!**s a defiant bubble.

"Weird," says Zed, wrinkling his nose. "Not sure I liked having all these strangers milling around. Specially awful ones like that Spencer and his mates."

"First days are often the worst days, don't forget," Lulu says, putting a hand on the shoulders of both her kids and giving them a squeeze. "It'll be better tomorrow, I'm positive."

"Maybe they were just feeling awkward being somewhere new and different," Arch tells Lulu. Maybe he's being extra-fair to these strangers to St Grizzle's, since HE was one till very, *very* recently. "And some of the Twits seemed really nice."

"Actually, that's true," I chip in, backing Arch up. "When everyone was clearing up after lunch, Granny Viv started chatting to them, and afterwards it felt like we were all less shy of each other."

"Your Granny Viv is VERY good at putting people at their ease," says Lulu, dropping her arms, grabbing her tossed shoes from the floor and beginning to stroll away. "Though I'm not so keen on her turning you lot into full-on clowns today of all days, when we had our visitors!"

"But I suppose it DID get the Twits' attention," Zed points out, as he turns his wheelchair and begins to follow his mum. "When Mr Puddock wasn't around, lots of them started asking us questions and seemed friendlier."

"They did, didn't they?" Arch agrees, stopping to take off his red nose and wriggle the tutu off his hips.

"And they were all quite a laugh when they were doing the circus skills stuff," Zed admits with a shrug of his shoulders.

"Yeah," I suppose that WAS kind of OK," Swan grudgingly agrees, too, "till Mr Puddock turned up and ordered all the Twits to the hall *immediately*."

"Hmm ... speaking of tricky people," says Lulu, clearly referring to the Twit head teacher, "I'd better go and think about ways to persuade Boo's parents to let her stay. Wish me luck!"

Lulu disappears down the corridor to the right, in the direction of her office. As she drifts away, so does Zed, heading off to his room.

"I'm going to do some drawing in the dorm,"

says Swan, padding towards the stairs – before veering towards the kitchen and adding, "*after* I get a biscuit, that is..."

So now it's just me and Arch. Maybe it's a good time to tell my best and lovely friend that I didn't think much of the advice he gave Boo at lunch.

Only he gets in first with a fun suggestion.

"Hey, Dani – fancy making a ... uh ... mini-movie?" he grunts, as he nearly tumbles over, his leg all tangled in the tutu he's trying to take off.

"Yes, definitely!" I say, grabbing hold of my friend to steady him as he gives the elasticated netting one last tug to wrestle it free from his ankle. "I've already had an idea. Maybe it could be about a REALLY horrible schoolboy who does mean stuff to everyone, and then the tables are turned."

"Ooh, I wonder who you based *that* on...?" Arch jokes, stroking his chin thoughtfully as I grin back at him. "Anyway, which of the ex-toys should we use for Spencer and his friends? Maybe they should all be plastic dinosaurs? What do you reckon, Dani? Dani?"

I'm only half-listening because my attention has been caught by something. A few scribbled somethings.

"Look," I mumble, pointing to the smiling staff photos on the wall.

Arch looks ... and sees the black-marker squiggles on some of them. Lulu, Miss Amethyst and Mademoiselle Fabienne now have bunny ears. Granny Viv has a moustache. As for poor Toshio, his photo's come off the worst – all his teeth have been blacked out and his eyes have been crossed.

It's GOT to be Spencer's handiwork, hasn't it? Didn't I just *guess* there'd be more meanness in store, courtesy of the most terrible of the Twits?

Uh-oh... At that **exact** moment, Toshio backs out of the boys' toilets, slopping and clunking a mop around on the floor. Arch's reflexes suddenly sharpen up – he grabs the vandalized photo off the wall and bundles it under his newly shaken-free tutu.

"Hi!" says Toshio, spotting us loitering. "There has been BIG accident here."

"What's happened?" I ask, walking closer.

"THIS has happened," he replies, pointing back inside the loos.

Oh... Half of Twittering School might have had  the river sloshing about its classrooms and corridors, but right now me and Arch are pretty surprised to see that St Grizzle's has a flooding problem of its own.

Arch walks closer still, sticks his head round the door of the boys' loos – and quickly pulls it out again, while leaning his hand on the brass doorknob.

"Hmm... Someone's 'accidentally' stuffed toilet paper in every plughole in every sink and 'accidentally' turned on all the taps," says Arch.

He raises his eyebrows at me. I raise mine back.

"Aargh!" my friend suddenly growls, peeling his hand away from the doorknob and finding it attached by a rubbery string of chewing gum that's been deliberately stuck there.

Seems like Spencer and his charming friends have been very busy indeed.

Right, this calls for a serious case of revenge...

Chapter 10
Random Acts of Stupidness

And snooping
and marshmallows...

Turns out, we're banned from ANY kind of revenge.

Even though I definitely saw Lulu's nostrils flare when me and Arch told her about the mini-lake in the loos and the other stuff.

"What's going on?" asks Zed, zooming into his mum's office so fast that the tyres on his wheelchair screech. His bedroom is right next door to Lulu's office – he must've overheard us moaning to his mum.

"Something up?" asks Swan, appearing in the doorway, too, with one of Granny Viv's homemade peanut-butter-choc-chip cookies in her hand.

"We found THIS," Arch announces, holding up poor, sweet Toshio's staff photo as evidence.

"Let me see that!" Swan snaps, grabbing the framed photo for a closer look. "Does Toshio know about it?"

"Uh, **no**," says someone who *isn't* me or Arch.

"Hello, Toshio..." Lulu smiles, and we all look round apologetically.

Whoops.

Our receptionist is standing in the doorway with the mop, his big white headphones wrapped round his neck.

"Someone has made a joke? For me?" he asks. His mouth is smiling but his eyes look hurt.

"A rotten one! Made by a rotten person!" snaps Swan, as she grabs a tissue out of the box on Lulu's desk and begins to rub at the glass of the picture frame. The black graffiti doesn't budge.

"It's not only Toshio's photo," I add, so our friends get the whole picture. "There were others. And the boys' toilets were deliberately flooded."

"Don't forget about the doorknob being gummed," says Arch.

Zed crinkles his freckly nose in irritation. Swan narrows her eyes, steam practically shooting out of her nostrils.

"OK. I KNOW it's infuriating, but before any of you start thinking of ways to get back at anyone," says Lulu, holding her hands up, "as I was JUST saying to Dani and Arch, we have no actual proof who did all this. And remember, Mr Puddock has made it clear that he doesn't intend for his Year 6s to stay at St Grizzle's for very long. So I think the best course of action is to hope the next few days go smoothly and that this is just a one-off."

"*Three*-off technically," Zed points out, counting the vandalized photos, the flooded toilets and the chewing-gum-on-the-doorknob on his fingers.

And that's not counting the horrible copy-catting of Toshio's accent, but I'm not going to mention that now, not while Toshio's standing here, already looking confused and hurt.

"So that's it? We just have to suck it up? No revenge?" says Swan, waving the photo in the air and sounding frustrated with her mum.

"No revenge," Lulu said very definitely – before she raises one eyebrow at us and smiles. "But perhaps we could have a little bit of security and snooping ... and marshmallows."

I swap glances with my friends, intrigued already.

Just what could Lulu have in mind?

Lulu decided that after a long day with (pesky) guests, we needed a Whole School Meeting this evening – and where better to have it than round the campfire, in the clearing in the woods, with a whole fortnight's worth of marshmallows, just because.

Actually, because she wanted an excuse for fun AND a chance to talk to everyone about the **security** and **snooping** business.

Not forgetting the sweet stuff.

"Hey, Lulu, back in your office earlier, I was TOTALLY confused when you mentioned the marshmallows!" says Arch, through a mouthful of toasted, er, marshmallows.

Me and Arch are sharing one of the smaller logs – with Boo squished between the sandwich of us bigger kids.

"He thought you meant we'd need them to throw at Spencer and his friends," I explain.

Lulu laughs so much the stick she's holding begins to shake and a marshmallow falls off the end and tumbles into the campfire, immediately turning into delicious-smelling burnt gloop.

"THIS might come in handy, though," says
Swan, wafting *her* stick around. "One false move
and Spencer gets it up the nose..."

Uh-oh. The Newts – who've refused to get
changed or wash their faces like the rest of us
– start brandishing their own marshmallow sticks
like a hoard of demented weeny clowns from a
horror movie. Specially since their face paint
has started to melt in the heat of the fire.

"Calm down, you lot," Granny Viv says

cheerfully, though she knows as well as we do that there's a slim chance of that. Still, she *tries* shooing the Newts back to their tree-trunk bench. And nope, it doesn't work – they've had too many marshmallows and gone sugar-loopy.

"So what's the plan, Ms Murphy?" Yas asks above the Newts' noise, while straightening the tea towel on her patch of tree trunk so that she doesn't get moss or bark on her neat school skirt.

"Yeah, what do you mean by 'security' and 'snooping'?" Klara quizzes our head teacher.

"With **security**, what I mean is teams of us should patrol the corridors and bathrooms over the next few days. That way no one can go wandering around unseen and get up to mischief," explains Lulu.

"I'll work out a rota," Miss Amethyst offers.

"Thank you," Lulu says with a nod. "As for **snooping** – well, I'd just like everyone to keep their eyes open for any random acts of stupidness."

Fnurrrppp!

Right on cue, a random *ringtone* of stupidity bursts out.

Immediately, we all look at Arch – but it's BOO who takes her phone out of her pocket.

"Like this?" she says, looking up at Arch as she presses the tiny 'off' button at the top.

"That's my girl!" Arch says approvingly, giving her the thumbs up.

I stare wide-eyed at my friend, wondering what he's playing at. It's one thing for him to ignore his OWN parents, but another to encourage Boo to do the same...

"Hey, Boo said she made some bird biscuits a little while ago?" says Arch, turning around to the whole of the campfire crew.

"Um, yes... I've got them here," says Granny Viv, reaching down to a big plastic tub by her feet. "They're Boo's first attempts at shortbread and I think they're rather wonderful. And they're still warm from the oven!"

Boo beams as the tub is passed around and everyone pulls out different-shaped, knobbly blobs. There are laughs and squeals and mad chatter as people try to guess what kind of bird *their* biscuitty blob is.

"An eagle!" claims May-Belle.

"Nightingale!" chirps Mademoiselle Fabienne.

"Owl?" guesses Toshio.

"Dodo!" Zed calls out.

"Swan?" suggests Swan.

The triplets just make the bird sounds instead.

"Is this one a penguin?" I ask Boo, when the tub comes round to me.

"Yes!" says Boo, her eyes lighting up. "I thought of making a penguin after seeing the one that pecked your mum's phone..."

Suddenly, Boo looks very sorry for herself again.

With everyone busy jumping and laughing and flying their biscuit birds around in crunchy flocks, I bend my head closer to Boo.

"Are you missing *your* mum?" I check with her.

"No... I'm just fed up because my mum and dad want to take me away from here!" she says miserably. "What if I get sent to a new school and they're not nice, Dani? What if no one teaches me how to make cookies, or wants to learn how to do bird noises? What if I'm not allowed to sleep in a cupboard? And what'll happen to Marvin?!"

"Hold on, I'll be right back," I say, and quickly get up.

Boo is getting herself in a complete pickle about her parents and I think it'll take *more* than me saying soothing things or Arch goofing around to make it better.

"What's up, Dani?" asks Lulu, once I wiggle and wend my way round the campfire and my bouncy, loud schoolmates and get to her side.

"Could you come over and talk to Boo?" I say quietly in her ear. "She's really worried that her parents are going to switch her to another school..."

"Ah, OK." Lulu nods, following me back round. "The truth is, Dani, Mr and Mrs Featherton-Snipe *were* dead set on her leaving, but I called them again a little while ago and persuaded them to think it over for the next few days. AND to talk it through with Boo."

"Well, *that* could be tricky, if she won't take their calls," I mumble, as we circle our way around the campfire and get back to Boo.

Lulu makes a "Hmm..." sort of noise before taking my spot on the tree trunk and sitting herself down beside Boo.

"So, sweetie," Lulu begins gently. "It looks as if you're **deliberately** missing phone calls from your mum and dad. I don't really think that's a good idea."

"Arch does!" Boo pipes up, sounding louder than usual in her burst of enthusiasm. "Arch says we're on strike! He says our parents are rubbish! He says we're all like a gang at St Grizzle's cos EVERYONE's parents are rubbish. Or they wouldn't have dumped their kids here and just gone off to have a good time!"

If anyone happened to have a pin and happened to drop it, we'd have heard it in the silence that's suddenly descended in the clearing.

Every Newt, Otter, Conker and Fungi is staring at Arch. Every member of staff, too. Only Downboy and Twinkle aren't staring, cos out of the corner of my eye I just spotted them running off with a packet of marshmallows each while everyone was distracted.

"Well, it's *kind* of true, isn't it?" Arch says sheepishly, just as a dumb noise parps from his phone.

UH-OH!

OK, so I know that's the ringtone Arch has set for his mum, but hey, it suits his **random act of stupidness** perfectly...

Chapter 11
Team Bonkers

And Old Age
Punks...

It's Tuesday morning and we've just picked up an ancient punk from the bus stop – in other words, Granny Viv's best friend Eric.

"Daisy's looking good, Viv!" says the older man, who's just swung himself into the passenger seat, after thunking his bag and guitar case into the back of the camper van. The silver metal of his multiple ear piercings glint in the sunlight.

"That's **it**? No, 'Hello, Viv, hello, Dani, hello, Arch'?" Granny Viv teases him.

"Hello, Viv, it's good to see you," says Eric, grinning as he remembers his manners. He turns to look over the back of the seat at me and MY best friend. "All right, Dani? Good to see you again. And how're you, Arch? Er ... not too good, by the looks of it!"

Eric's right. Arch isn't too good. Not after saying what he said last night. Not after being shunned by every pupil except ME ever since, and I'M pretty cross with him, too.

In fact my friend is folded up on the seat beside me, as if he's an unhappy piece of origami, as if he's trying to disappear.

"I said something stupid last night and now no one's talking to me," Arch mumbles from under his baseball cap and over the top of his knees, which he's clutching to his chest.

"No one … like your mates, you mean?" asks Eric, shooting a questioning glance at me.

"No one, like no one at ALL," Arch mumbles.

"Wow. So, kid, you're telling me that you've managed to make an *entire school's worth of people* annoyed with you?" says Eric, with raised grey bushy eyebrows. "That is REALLY impressive!"

"I didn't *mean* to make everyone cross," Arch says sorrowfully. "I've tried telling them I'm sorry. Lots of times."

He has.

"But it hasn't worked…"

It hasn't.

"Well, no wonder, Arch!" I burst in. "It was **bad enough** saying everyone's parents were rubbish. It was **bad enough** that you said everyone had been 'dumped' at St Grizzle's. But THEN you said it was because their mums and dads were off having a 'good time'...? That was **bad**, Arch."

"Well, Angel's parents DO look like they're having a good time in their Bollywood movies," Arch says in a small voice, as he tries to justify himself.

"They don't just dance and sing for a few minutes, then knock off for the day!" I snap at my friend, thumping his arm for good measure. "They're sometimes filming on location for weeks at a time."

"Oh..." Arch mumbles.

"*May-Belle*'s parents tour with their country band eight months of the year, *Yas*'s dad is a busy diplomat abroad somewhere, the *triplets*' parents are in Africa working for a charity, *Klara*'s parents are off around the world lecturing, *my* mum's on an expedition in the South Pole," I say, counting just a few examples off on my fingers. "And BLOSSOM's dad is in the army in Afghanistan, so he's not exactly having a 'good time', is he? DO you want me to carry on?"

"No..." Arch says in the small voice again.

I'm kind of glad he doesn't need more proof. I have no idea what the rest of the Newts' parents do for work – I can't even remember what most of the Newts *names* are. But I've made my point.

"The thing is, Arch," Granny Viv takes over, as she drives along, her big earrings swaying whenever we take a left or right, "sometimes parents aren't perfect."

She's making a good point. I didn't think Mum was very perfect when she chose the Antarctica expedition over me.

"True!" adds Eric, nodding at Granny Viv.

"In fact, there ARE times when even the most perfect parents have to make *im*perfect choices."

I'm impressed – that was quite poetic for a shouty punk singer. But yes, parents might have to make imperfect choices, like sending their kids to boarding school, I suppose.

"Exactly. Difficult choices aren't always popular," Granny Viv carries on, "but often they're the right thing to do in the long run. Do you see what I mean?"

Granny Viv gazes at Arch in the rear-view mirror.

Gulp. I don't think Granny Viv is just talking about grown-ups choosing to send their children away to boarding school. I think she's *also* talking about grown-ups having to do tricky things – like break up.

I think Arch gets that, too... His hand has crept over to mine and I give his fingers a best-friend squeeze.

"But anyway, sounds like you might need a helping hand sorting out the situation with your schoolmates, Arch," Granny Viv continues, in more of a let's-get-on-with-it voice. "We'll have to have a think about ways that can happen, eh, Dani?"

"Definitely," I say, still holding my friend's hand.

Actually, I currently have a short but important **Wrongs to Put Right** list:

1) Help Arch make up with everyone

2) Get Arch talking to his parents

3) Figure out how Boo can stay at St Grizzle's

4) Pay sneery Spencer back for his meanness towards Toshio.

But trying to figure out *that* lot makes my brain suddenly feel as tangly as the wire on stored-away fairy lights...

"First things first, though," announces Granny Viv. "Let's get back and see what's going on at St Grizzle's!"

Actually, I know exactly what's going on back at school right now – the Year 6 Twits will be doing their normal morning lessons with Mr Nayar. However, 'normal' morning lessons for the Newts, Otters, Conkers and Fungi have been suspended ... in favour of a mega-school-tidy-thon. A still smartly dressed Lulu wants the school to be SPOTLESS and IMPRESSIVE for the Huddleton Retirement Lodge residents, village-school parents, important councillors and local journalists who'll be in the audience of '**Keep Calm and Carry On**' tonight.

So there are several teams doing several jobs.

Team 1: Lulu, Miss Amethyst, Swan and the Conkers are tidying, preening and beautifying every speck of the school and gardens that they can.

Team 2: Toshio, Zed and assorted Newts are roaming the corridors, on the lookout for any mischief happening around hidden corners.

Team 3: Mademoiselle Fabienne, the triplets and Boo are picking and arranging flowers, and then baking like crazy baking people.

As for us, we're **Team 4**... Granny Viv took me and Arch along with her to the village supermarket to help get drinks and nibbly bits for the visitors tonight – and just happened to time her trip to coincide with the arrival of the bus that Eric was on. And mess monsters Twinkle and Downboy are in **Team 4**, too, just to keep them out of the way.

"Ooh, LOOK!" Granny Viv says suddenly, flicking on Daisy's clicketty-clacketty indicator and pulling over. "It's Neville! Roll down the window, Eric! HELLO, NEVILLE! Remember us from the Twittering School Fair on Sunday afternoon? From the **Splat Stall**?"

A smiling Neville thunks on the brakes of his motorized scooter and tips his natty hat at Granny Viv.

"How could I forget a pretty face like yours?" he says in his most charming voice.

An older lady walking beside him leans on her cherry-patterned wheelie shopping trolley and rolls her eyes.

"Don't take any notice of Neville," she says good-naturedly. "He's like this to ALL the women at Huddleton Lodge."

"Oh, you adore me really, Stella," says Neville, waving her comments away. "Anyway, how is that lovely little girl after what happened at the fair? Not too upset by those awful big children, I hope?"

"She's fine, thanks," says Granny Viv, leaning right across Eric. "By the way, do any of you need a lift to St Grizelda's for the show tonight? I've got Daisy here or the school minibus, and will happily be your chauffeur!"

"Well, that's very kind, but I think we're all fixed," says Neville. "Still, now that you mention the show, can I ask you something?"

"Sure!" says Granny Viv. "Fire away!"

"They're calling it '**Keep Calm and Carry On**' ... which I know is a very popular phrase these days. On posters and mugs and what have you," says Neville, rubbing his short beard. "The thing is, it's originally a wartime slogan. PLEASE tell me these Twitty kids aren't going to be singing awful old wartime songs?"

Me and Arch exchange glances. Uh-oh.

"Young folk seem to think we'll like that stuff," Stella jumps in before Granny Viv can answer. "But most of us living at the Lodge were just babies during the war, so we're not too keen on those old-fashioned tunes!"

"Yes, we were teenagers in the fifties and sixties," says Neville. "We like rock 'n' roll! Elvis Presley! Chuck Berry!"

"What about ska?" Eric chips in, leaning across Granny Viv and sounding very keen now that music was being mentioned.

"Ska!" Neville repeats. "Oh, my days, how I liked to twist and turn to that!"

"'Ska'?" Arch mouths at me, and I shrug back. Whatever 'ska' is, I don't think it's got anything to do with birds flying over cliffs or rabbits run, run running.

"Ooh, it was the Beatles for me!" Stella sighs happily, and begins to dance with her wheelie shopping trolley as a partner. "*Oh, love, love me DO...!*"

"Uh-oh ... look what we've done – we've set her off!" Neville laughs as Stella sings. He joins in, too, driving his motorized scooter in a figure of eight.

"Ha! No, no – of *course* the show's not going to be all stuffy old wartime songs," says Granny Viv, raising her voice as she reassures them. "Anyway, better go. See you tonight!"

With that, she winds the window up fast.

"What do we do now?" I ask, holding on tight to my seat belt as Granny Viv flicks on the clicketty-clacketty indicator and veers off fast.

"We go talk to the Head Twit!" she announces.

"The *who* now?" asks Eric, probably regretting he's come, since he's apparently part of Team Bonkers.

But Granny Viv is too busy thinking to answer. She turns one corner, then another, then screeches to a stop outside Twittering School.

And *there* is the Head Twit – shouting at a man in a yellow safety helmet. He stops when he catches sight of the purple, flowery cuteness that is Daisy, though.

"Hello! Hi, Mr Puddock – can I have a quick word?" Granny Viv calls, as she jumps out of the camper van, with me, Arch and an elderly punk following after her.

"What are you doing here?" demands a frowning Mr Puddock. He doesn't know whether to stare at Granny Viv or the colourful van.

KEEP OFF
THE GRASS

"Look, we just bumped into some of the residents from Huddleton Lodge," says Granny Viv. "And the thing is, they don't LIKE wartime songs. So I'm thinking that means tonight's show will have to be tweaked."

"*Tweaked?*" Mr Puddock splutters, his grey cheeks flushing pink spots of rage. "Well, that is NOT going to happen. We most certainly will NOT change a thing on a whim, Ms Er…"

"Viv, her name's Viv," Eric snarls at Mr Puddock. I can almost imagine him with the skyscraping Mohican hairdo Granny Viv told me he wore when he was seventeen. (Eric has only enough hair for a mini-Mohican now.)

"But—" Granny Viv tries again, and is silenced by one of Mr Puddock's hand slices.

"Madam, I have no time for this nonsense. And with inspectors coming and an urgent meeting in the town hall to attend, I can't even be at St Grizelda's for today's dress rehearsal. So tell Mr

Nayar *he's* in charge, and that I've sent over all the costumes in a taxi. And tell him to do it JUST AS IT IS, and that I'll see him at the show tonight. Understood?"

"Understood!" says Granny Viv, clicking together the heels of her chunky shoes and giving Mr Puddock a sarcastic salute.

"So that's it, then?" I say, as we all bundle back inside the van. "Neville and his friends will have to sit through that awful show?"

"What are you talking about, Dani?" Granny Viv smiles at me in the rear-view mirror as we zip back on the road again. "Of COURSE we're not going to inflict that boring mess on those lovely people. Once me and Lulu put our heads together, we'll figure out a fun way to save this show. With a little help from our friends, of course! Eh, Eric?"

"No problem," Eric replies with a grin and a crack of his knuckles before he turns around to face us. "Could one of you guys shoo the goat off my case and grab my guitar?"

As I do the shooing and Arch does the grabbing, we look at each other and KNOW tonight is going to be ... well, not QUITE what Mr Puddock might be expecting.

Yesssss!

And then a light bulb of an idea pops into my head, just as I duck to avoid the gently twanging guitar being passed over my head.

The idea? It's actually *nothing* to do with rejigging the show and *everything* to do with No. 1 on my **Wrongs to Put Right List**...

Chapter 12
A Whole Gazillion of Surprises

And Arch's sorry song...

Granny Viv is a genius.

Not only have she and Lulu managed to swizzle the show around at this very late stage, but she also flattered Swan into being the host for this evening's new-look performance by telling her she's the most grown-up person in the school. (She probably is. And the grumpiest, but let's not talk about that.)

And now she's managed to sort out JUST the right ratio of margherita to pepperoni pizza to keep all the pupils of Twittering and St Grizzle's happy at the pre-show tea.

Of course, there's other stuff that Granny Viv's genius at, but I'll get to that...

"E.Y.U., Dani!" says Swan, gliding into the dining hall, looking a little like a ballet dancer in her black T-shirt, leggings and pink tutu.

As she's doing the important job of being the host, one of the triplets added a tiara (free from the front of a magazine) to her long black hair.

Its sparkly plastic diamonds look properly posh.

"E.Y.U. back at you!" I say, slapping the hand she holds out to me before she slides into a chair and grabs a slice of pizza.

I'm on the technical team (with Arch, Boo and Toshio), so I'm in my normal clothes with a tutu on top. Basically, a tutu on top is the regulation uniform for tonight, whatever the rest of people's outfits happen to be.

"What's EE-WHY-YOU?" Blossom demands through a mouthful of pizza.

Like the rest of the Newts, she's opted for full clown make-up, a tutu and Afghani bells for the show, and has added her own personal touch – a pair of wobbling deely boppers on her head for extra pizzazz.

Since Swan is mid-snack, I answer Blossom's question.

"It's what Lulu decided the show should be about," I tell her, remembering how enthusiastic Lulu got when Granny Viv explained how necessary it was to change the performance. "E.Y.U. stands for 'Embrace Your Uniqueness'."

Blossom looks over at Lulu, who's smiling and chatting with some Twits, then blinks blankly at me, the way she does when Toshio sometimes forgets he's actually talking in Japanese and not English. Or when someone tries to explain to her and the rest of the Newts that shoving all your clothes under your bed doesn't make it a wardrobe.

"It means being different is GOOD," I spell out to Blossom. "Lulu said that is exactly what St Grizzle's is all about. What every school should be about."

"EE-WHY-YOU..." Blossom mutters

thoughtfully. "Am I one of those? A YOU-NEEK-ER?"

"Yes, you absolutely *are* unique, Blossom," I say with a very, very firm nod.

Actually, the whole of today has been pretty unique, ever since we got back from the village.

There have been lightning-fast auditions in front of Miss Amethyst, Mademoiselle Fabienne and Mr Nayar. At first, the Twits' Year 6 teacher HAD looked a bit uncertain and uncomfortable when Lulu and Granny Viv told him about their hijack plans for '**Keep Calm and Carry On**', but he got totally on board with it all once they explained it was:

a) in a good cause (ie not boring the Huddleton Lodge audience to death), and

b) going to be insanely good fun.

Apart from the auditions, there's been busyness in every corner of the school. Cakes have been baked, lighting tested, music practised, dances rehearsed and costumes thrown together or adapted in the case of the uniforms Mr Puddock had taxied over.

Me and Arch even had time to sneak off and quickly make a mini-movie.

And nope, our schoolmates *still* aren't talking to Arch, but at least everyone's been so incredibly busy that there hasn't been toooo much time for hurt scowls and growls...

"This has been the BEST DAY EVER!" announces a Twit called Jessica, who happens to be the most amazing tap dancer. She's been frantically rehearsing her piece on the kitchen flagstones, making the most excellent racket. As she speaks, she waves a piece of pepperoni pizza in the air like a celebration flag.

It has not been the best day ever for Spencer and his friends.

Earlier on, Swan pointed out to Lulu, Granny Viv and Mr Nayar that Spencer might JUST be the sort of person to try and get in touch with Mr Puddock and tell him about the changes that were happening to the show – which could ruin everything.

It was decided that he and his idiot friends needed to be kept well out of the way till the latest possible time… That's when Granny Viv came up with *another* genius plan. Knowing that Spencer and co would never take an order from her, she asked a very willing Mr Nayar to instruct them that all one hundred of the folding chairs stacked in the hall cupboards needed to be washed and polished dry. (They didn't.)

Spencer and his buddies were out there on the back lawn with the hosepipe and sponges and cloths for HOURS this afternoon. (Boo, being lovely, took them some of her newly made cake and squash. Not that they deserved it.)

And now that they've brought in and set up all the chairs in the hall, and are sitting down in the dining room having pizza with everyone, it's finally clicked with them – SOMETHING IS WEIRD.

"Hey, what's with all this glitter?" says the tall one with the sticky-up hair, frowning around the room at all the sparkly cheeked faces beaming back at him. His name is Kyle. Now that we've got to know all the other (nice) Twits, we found out the names of Spencer's crew AND the fact that the (nice) Twits don't like them much either.

"Was glitter even IN the war?" asks the pointy-faced girl (Abi).

"Nah," mutters the boy who chews gum dopey-cow-style. (He is called Mason. He chews his pizza the same way.) "Neither were those frilly little pink skirts…"

"What's happening? Why are the Grizzlers dressed up, too?" asks Spencer, gazing around in confusion. "And where's Mr Puddock? Hasn't he arrived yet?"

"Aw, are you missing him, Spender? That's sweet," says Granny Viv, popping more pizzas down on the tables, for everyone to help themselves.

"It's **Spencer**," says Spencer, narrowing his eyes at her.

"Whatever," Granny Viv says with a shrug, just as Lulu wanders over.

"You know Mr Puddock's been stuck in important meetings all day," Lulu says to Spencer, her smile full beam and slightly fake. "But don't worry – he's on his way. As for the St

Grizelda students being dressed up... Well, I decided to tweak the show just a **tiny** bit, to include them, too."

"But that's not fair! It's OUR show," Spencer bleats, glancing around again. "And wait a minute – have some of them taken our parts? Cos me and Kyle and Abi and Mason haven't rehearsed at all today and—"

"Now don't panic," Lulu interrupts, patting Spencer quite *hard* on the shoulder. "Mr Nayar already explained that you and your friends were SO good you didn't need to rehearse any more."

"And you and your friends will be performing the *exact* same songs, Spender," adds Granny Viv. "We promise."

Spencer looks at Granny Viv warily, not sure he can trust her. Which he can't, really.

"Only you're going to have a *real-live guitarist* playing the tunes for you, rather than a backing track. Won't that be a treat?" Lulu says brightly.

"Ah, and here he is now!"

Right on cue, Eric meanders into the dining hall, wearing a slogan T-shirt, ripped jeans and his guitar strapped across his chest. He sticks a mini-amp down on a table.

Spencer's eyebrows immediately wrinkle into two caterpillars of confusion.

"Er ... what's Granny Viv's friend doing?" asks Zed, suddenly zipping up alongside me.

"You'll see," I say with a secret smile on my face.

I glance over at Granny Viv, who knows exactly what's coming next, since I suggested it in the camper van this morning. It was a way for Arch's apology to be heard, loud and clear, by his St Grizzle's schoolmates. (Tonight's show isn't the ONLY thing that's been rehearsed behind closed classroom doors. And Granny Viv isn't the ONLY genius in the family.)

Everyone sits to attention, open-mouthed, as

Eric clangs an ear-splitting chord.

Knowing that's his cue, Arch bangs in through the dining-room door, a microphone in his hand. Boo is by his side, practically bouncing with excitement and holding a sheet with lyrics for him to sing.

"Huh?" I see Swan's mouth move, though any noise at all in the room is drowned out by the racket of the song.

"To everyone at St Grizzle's, can I say sorry?
If you don't believe me
I'll only just worry.
Please forgive me and
know I'm so sorry,
Cos you all know that
I'm a numpty now
A great big numpty
who's sorry
nowwwww!"

The song is loosely inspired by Justin Bieber's hit 'Sorry', but since it's been rewritten (by me) and punkified (by Eric), I'm not sure anyone would recognize it.

But it works like I hoped it would. Everyone's laughing and forgetting to be cross with Arch because he quite clearly and *fabulously* CAN'T SING.

I watch as the scared, will-this-work look on my best friend's face changes to a beaming smile of relief.

Hope Arch is still smiling later, if I manage to make No. 2 on the **Wrongs to Put Right List** happen.

Which reminds me – if I am going to make it happen, I need to ping a quick text now...

Chapter 13
Tutu Much Fun

And a shock splat...

"Wow, SHE'S looking pretty fabulous!" says Arch, staring up at St Grizzle.

It's true. Our beloved statue has a glamorous pink feather boa draped dramatically round her shoulders.

"Marvin approves," I say, nodding at Boo's pet pigeon, who's perched in St Grizzle's left hand, gently cooing at the arriving guests. He seems unbothered by the bells dangling from St Grizzle's fingers, softly chiming in the evening summer breeze.

"Ha ha! Is this one of those living statues?" someone asks.

It's Neville, crunching over the gravel in his motorized scooter. His friend Stella and some more people who must be Huddleton Lodge residents are ambling up the driveway behind him.

"Only the bird part," I tell Neville, as I watch Marvin flutter his wings and do a delicate little poo.

"Well, THIS place is very nice!" says Neville,

glancing around. "Never been here before!"

That's what most of the guests have been saying, **"oohing"** and **"aahing"** at the beautiful old building. I spotted Spencer's mum a few minutes ago, with a baby-bouncing man who must be his dad. (The matching quiff was a dead giveaway.)

"BEND DOWN!" Blossom suddenly orders Neville, appearing from nowhere with a paper garland on a string. Neville blinks at her but does as he's told and Blossom slips the floral necklace over his head. "THERE! It's called a LEI. It means WELCOME. It's what they do in a place called HOW-EYE-EYE!"

"Hawaii," I correct her gently, as I gaze around at the other lei-wearing guests. They are all milling about and chatting in front of the school, where wonky classroom tables are covered with pretty Indian throws (all borrowed from Miss Amethyst's bedroom), and laden with drinks, crisps and other nibbles. Zed and Toshio are in smart, waiter uniform of white top, black trousers and tutus. Toshio is bowing at guests and being very sociable – ie his headphones are round his neck rather than slapped over his ears.

Disappointingly, I can't see certain guests I've specially invited … but I CAN see Lulu, in a floaty hippy dress, standing with Mr Puddock and the town Mayor. Swan says her mum's done an EXCELLENT job of keeping the Head Twit talking to important people ever since he arrived, which meant Mr Puddock hasn't been inside and hasn't got a whiff of his show's mad makeover…

"Ladies and gentlemen!" we hear Swan's voice boom out now, from the front steps of the school. "My name is Swan Chen-Murphy, and on behalf of St Grizelda's School we are pleased to welcome you to a VERY special show tonight. You are about to see SO much talent, from the Year 6s of Twittering School AND the students here."

"Hey, check out Mr Puddock," says Arch, nudging me. "He looks like he's about to choke on his cocktail sausage."

The Head Twit certainly does, and he starts coughing, too, when he hears what Swan has to say next.

"This show might not be what you expect, but I PROMISE it's going to be very entertaining, celebrating the unique talents of all these amazing young people!"

There's a smattering of applause and a babble of excitement as the audience follows Swan into the building's impressively large, wood-panelled entrance hall. But if they were expecting to be ushered on through to take their seats in the *main* hall, they're wrong.

"Please gather here!" Swan calls out, as the earnest, red-nosed triplets neatly herd our guests into a semicircle at the foot of the grand staircase.

I can just see Boo, hunkered behind the banister, a remote control in her hand. Her eyes are fixed somewhere above, as if she's waiting for a signal. She is. And the signal involves a goat.

"*Now!*" we hear someone hiss from up on the first floor.

Boo presses 'play', and a jolly brass band intro strikes up.

 On that cue, Twinkle is released and comes trit-trotting down the flight of stairs, dressed in a pair of fairy wings and carrying/crunching a wand in her mouth.

Ripples of laughs and "aww"s ring out, and

I hear Stella yelp, "Oh, I know this! It's the Beatles' 'All You Need Is Love'!"

"*Love, love, love...*" the famous band begin to croon on the track.

"*LOVE, LOVE, LOVE...!*" roars a chorus of voices from the Huddleton residents.

Then there are gasps as Jessica the dancing Twit comes expertly tip-tapping down the stairs to the tune. She is dressed in a blazer, bow tie and tutu, and is accompanied on a lead by my very own fluffball Downboy, who is:

a) wearing a light-up, red flashing love-heart collar, and

b) practically smiling at the now wildly "awwing" crowd.

Well, the opener of the show is DEFINITELY a hit, DEFINITELY a surprise, DEFINITELY a genius idea of my gran's (told you) and DEFINITELY a bit of a TA-DAH! moment. And there're **plenty** more TA-DAH!s where that came from.

We've just got to make sure they come thick and fast, leaving Mr Puddock **no** time to catch his breath and protest.

"Come on," says Arch, tugging my sleeve as we wiggle through the crowds to get to the hall and our position operating lights and sound via the laptop set up in there...

Ushered by Swan, the audience follow us and are met by the sight of Angel doing a display of Bollywood dancing in front of a film snippet of her mum and dad shaking and shimmying along 'with' her.

The audience haven't even stopped whooping at that when they're hit next with a medley of the dreaded wartime tunes. But with silly costumes and super-fast punk riffs courtesy of Eric, the Twittering Year 6 performers are having a ball, and suddenly the songs come to life, sounding so pop that even Blossom's soldier dad might like them. It's a shame that Spencer seems especially sulky and is the only one of his friends not to dress up.

Now that old songs have been sung in a shiny new way, it's time for a demonstration of impressive brainpower. Two Twits called Leila and Mohammed – along with St Grizzle's own Yas and Boo – take to the stage and all four do a lightning-quick and frankly **staggering** test of mental maths, with Lulu firing the questions at them like a zookeeper chucking fish at hungry penguins.

The audience gasp at all the high-speed smartness and are only just catching their breath when Saheed, a Twit with a great voice, jumps on stage and bursts into big hit 'Happy'. Within seconds, he has the whole audience clapping along, while the clown-faced Newts dance and jingle-jangle behind him, playing the toy musical instruments Granny Viv discovered in her cupboard tidy the other night.

"Thank you, Saheed and the Red Nosers!" says Swan, leading the clapping as the stage empties and the huge whiteboard glides down. "Now in a few minutes, we'll be moving outdoors for the NEXT part of our show. But before that, I'd like to present a short example of stop-frame animation, by expert film-makers Dani Dexter and Arch Kaminski!"

Me and Arch give each other a quick grin, super-proud of our frantically planned and filmed mini-movie. There are four 'characters' in it, made up (mostly) of actors we found in the **Soft Toy Tombola** haul in the Newts' dorm.

"Here goes," I mutter, as I turn round to give Toshio a wave, over by the far wall. He's grinning because he's seen our film already and very much approves of it.

As the hall darkens, Arch presses 'play' on the screen of the school's laptop. A title flashes up on the whiteboard:

'Famous Last Words'

As that fades, the scene opens to show a big, squishy crested penguin, a cuddly, chunky Highland cow and a little, grey felt mouse. They are crowded around an egg (nicked from the fridge), with a mean sneery face drawn on it and a swoop of moulted goat fur glued to the top – quiff-style.

"Do you think they'll recognize themselves?" Arch whispers, talking of course about Kyle, Mason, Abi and – last and certainly least – Spencer.

"Do we care?" I whisper back, grinning.

"Er, I guess not – not one bit!" Arch sniggers.

In the dark, for just a split second I stare at Arch, wondering what he's going to think of the surprise I've got planned for him, if the surprise ever arrives...

But my little bubble of worry is popped as some cool music begins to play. The four characters in our film mooch across some grass towards the camera.

"It's great being us, isn't it?" says the sneery egg in the middle. (Voiced brilliantly by Arch.)

The penguin, cow and mouse grunt and squeak in agreement. (Me, Arch and Boo voicing together.)

"We're like the bosses of *everyone*, aren't we?" the egg announces.

More grunts and squeaks.

"*Me* especially," says the smug egg, inching closer to the camera. "Right?"

"Right!" the furry others chip in.

"*No one* stops me from doing what I want to do," the egg boasts.

"Yay!" cheer the egg's chums.

"I get up to all sorts and *never* get caught," sneers the egg, rolling ever closer to the camera. "Do I?"

"No!" the chums cheer on.

"And if anyone's got a problem with that then I *dare* you to take a walk over to me and—"

Out of nowhere, a giant foot in a trendy trainer thuds down – **instantly** squashing the egg and **instantly** making the audience BURST into surprised laughter.

Then a huge, dark haired head tips into the frame.

"Oops!" says a grinning Toshio.

'The End'

The whooping and roaring – led by Granny Viv – fills the whole hall. Even the performers seem to have slipped out from the wings in the dark so that they could watch the film, and are now clapping madly.

"That went down pretty well," I mutter to Arch as the lights go back up. "Look – even Spencer's mum and dad are laughing!"

His poor parents obviously don't have a clue how sneaky their son is. Or how much he deserved to be No. 4 on my **Wrongs to Put Right List**, and be paid back for all his meanness this week and every other week.

"It didn't go down well with one particular person, of course," says Arch, pointing over to a huddle of students sitting cross-legged on the floor. Spencer looks so fuming with rage that I expect to see steam coming out of his ears. But he's not just mad at our mini-movie – he's livid with his crew, who are bent over laughing too much to notice...

And no surprise, but it doesn't seem as if Mr Puddock has much of a sense of humour. I've just spotted the Head Twit clapping reluctantly and looking confused about what everyone is finding so funny.

"Wasn't that egg-cellent?" Swan booms into the microphone, then winces. "Sorry, that was my twin brother's bad joke. Anyway, if everyone could follow me…"

Uh-oh. As the audience begins squeaking and shuffling along the rows of chairs, I see a quiff pointing our way above the crowds and glimpse a hint of a glower. I guess Spencer's figuring out if he can get me and Arch back for that very public put-down.

No chance, Spencer.

After our campfire-and-marshmallow meeting last night, all of us at St Grizzle's are a crack unit of snoopers and security, and one of us has always got our eye on him.

There will be no more stupid Spencer shenanigans – not on our watch!

Chapter 14
Shenanigans Happen

And everyone congas!

"TWIT TWOOOOOO!"

"I thought she's supposed to be a bat?" says Boo, watching as Blossom swings upside down on the trapeze to the **"wow"**s of the watching crowd below.

"She is," I confirm, looking at the pair of bat wings Blossom added to her mismatched clown/tutu costume right before she scampered up the rope ladder a few minutes ago. "I don't think she's so sure what noise bats make. Maybe you need to teach her bat songs? Same as you've been teaching the triplets to—"

"Ooh!" Boo gasps, as if I've reminded her of something. "Got to get ready!"

In the golden light of the evening sun, Boo scurries off across the back lawn in the direction of the woods and the clearing. Watching her go, I sigh a little sigh.

Cos, yes, I've successfully ticked off No. 1 and 4 on my **Wrongs to Put Right List**. And maybe, hopefully, No. 2 might happen soon, if I keep my fingers super-tightly crossed. But what about No. 3? I'm still no closer to figuring out how Boo can stay at St Grizzle's – what if her parents have already decided that enough is enough and are right this second trying to telephone Lulu?

"What's Boo up to?" asks Zed.

With no sound and lighting to worry about for a little while, me and Arch have been able to hang out with Zed and cheer on the displays of assorted footballing trick-shots, gymnastic bendiness and circus fandango-ing from a jumble of enthusiastic St Grizzle's and Twittering students.

"Boo's got to round up her little birds," I joke.

"She won't find them in the trees right now," says Zed, nodding over to a picnic bench where the triplets are sitting with Toshio, all companionably stuffing themselves with sausage rolls.

"Don't you think Toshio looks a bit different?" Zed suddenly muses, tilting his head to gaze at our receptionist.

"Maybe it's the smart clothes. Or the tutu," Arch suggests. "Or the fact that he looks like a hamster with all that food in his mouth."

"Nah ... it's because he's not wearing his big headphones," I chip in, thinking our receptionist looks super-weird without them. I remember him lending them to Boo when she was operating the lighting earlier on in the show. They're probably still lying beside the computer back in the main hall.

"Thank you, Blossom!" we hear Swan call out on her microphone, with an answering "TWIT

TWOO!" floating above her. "Now it's time for the finale of tonight's show. So could everyone please follow Klara..."

With a gasp-worthy series of cartwheels, Klara sets off towards the clearing in the woods with everyone laughing and chatting and strolling after her.

It gives me a second to scour the faces in the crowds ... but nope, I still don't see who I want to see. Falling back from my friends, I wriggle my phone out of my pocket and sneak a peek at it.

Yay! There's a text.

Traffic jam on motorway – might not make it!

No! When did this come through? My mobile's been on silent...

"Come on!" Arch calls out over his shoulder, wondering why I've slowed down and waving me to catch up with him and Zed. I shove my phone back in my pocket and slap a smile on my face

– even though I'm frowning inside.

When we get to the clearing, Granny Viv has the campfire ready and glowing. There are folding chairs around the tree trunks and rugs spread out on the ground for the non-performing performers to lounge on, too.

"Listen, can you hear beautiful birdsong?" says Swan, tipping a hand to her ear once everyone is settled.

As the pretty tweeting begins, the audience glances up this way and that, only to "ahh!" when they suddenly spot the triplets trilling dainty bird sounds from the window of the nearby tree house. Perched on the walkway, with Marvin on the handrail beside her, Boo calls out the name of every feathered friend the triplets are impersonating.

Ripples of applause meet every sweet note and I spot Granny Viv filming the girls with a great red-lipped smile on her face.

As the last tweet rings out, Mademoiselle Fabienne begins to strum and sing a song called 'Blackbird', which Eric told me was *also* by the Beatles, when I came upon her rehearsing in the dining room earlier. I see that Mr Nayar is holding her music for her as delicately as if he was holding her heart.

The singing is so very pretty that tissues are being rustled from bags and eyes are being dabbed.

But oh … my heart suddenly **badda-booms** when I see Neville's friend Stella hand a tissue to the snuffling woman standing behind her seat.

It's gone all dusky and dreamlike here in the woods so I hadn't seen her arrive, or the man beside her.

I'm guessing the text I saw was from quite a while ago and that the traffic jam cleared.

And I'm also guessing that Mrs Kaminski is NOT crying at the pretty, sad-sounding song. She's crying because my best friend has just spotted his parents and gone bolting over to hug both of them…

Seems like I can safely tick off No. 3 on the **Wrongs to Put Right List**!

"Thank you ALL for coming tonight," I hear Swan announce, as the music dies away. "I hope you enjoyed yourselves as much as we did."

Cheers roar out. The mayor "Hear, hear!"s at the top of his deep voice, and is echoed enthusiastically by Neville and Spencer's dad, among others.

"And of course this wouldn't have been possible without two very important people," Swan carries on, "who made this event possible in their own, er, particular ways... Our head teachers, Mr Puddock and Lulu!"

Caught out, Mr Puddock looks perplexed at both the thank you and the applause that follows. He manages a half-smile and a nod of his head.

But Lulu immediately pings upright and stands on the tree stump she's been sitting on.

"Thanks, everyone!" she calls out cheerfully. "I really hope you enjoyed our show, which celebrated the uniqueness of every child at Twittering and St Grizelda's. And this show wouldn't have happened without the friendship that developed between us all. Put it there, friend!"

Lulu bounds off
her stump and holds a
hand out to a
completely flummoxed
Mr Puddock – who
limply lets his hand be
taken and shaken.

"But we're not
QUITE finished yet,"
Swan shouts above the
latest outburst of cheers and
clapping. "It's a song request from
Lulu – and pretty appropriate in the
circumstances. 'With a Little Help From my
Friends', by the Beatles!"

The whoops and squeeees are nearly as
deafening as the song that Eric and Mademoiselle
Fabienne start thrashing out together.

"This is AMAZING!" I hear Neville shout at
Mr Puddock. "Can we do it every week?"

I don't hear what Mr Puddock stutters in reply – I'm too focused on Arch and his mum and dad, who are now lost in a group hug under the sheltering branches of an oak. From the look on their faces, I think they're all a muddle of sad and happy and hopeful. I think that mix means they'll be OK, whatever happens.

"Dani?" says a small voice, and I realize a hand has slipped into mine.

I gaze down into Boo's wide eyes and my heart goes **squelch**. Who knows if things will work out OK for Arch's mini-me? If only I could've ticked off everything on my **Wrongs to Put Right** list today…

"Can I show you the mini-movie Granny Viv did?" asks Boo, holding up my gran's mobile. "She's a very good student!"

"Well, Boo's a very good teacher," says Granny Viv, coming to join us. "Want to have a look at my handiwork, Dani?"

As everyone around us jigs to the music –
which has now swapped to 'Jailhouse Rock' by Elvis
to Neville's cheer of approval – we three sit down
on a tree trunk and huddle around the phone.

A title flashes up: '**The Many Talents of
Boudicca Featherton-Snipe**'.

Next on the screen comes a quick-fire
collection of moments which ALL star Boo.

- Boo reading to the captivated Newts.
- Boo painstakingly explaining to Granny Viv
how to film and edit on a phone.
- Boo holding up a completed maths sheet in
class, while everyone groans, "What? Already?
HOW?"
- Boo getting a round of applause in circus skills
for mastering juggling with lemons (either
Downboy or Twinkle ate the official juggling
balls).
- Boo smiling as her classmates pick out her
birdie biscuit blobs.

- Boo proudly icing much-improved, delicious-looking cupcakes today.
- Boo testing the speakers and the sound before the opening tap sequence on the stairs.
- Boo on stage, being cheered alongside her fellow brainiac Yaz and the pair of Twits.
- Boo taking a bow with her birdsong buddies.
- Boo snuggled and asleep in her cupboard, surrounded by glimmers of fairy lights, illuminating all the books she's stacked up on the shelves. It looks like she's sleeping in the most magical library ever...

And on a freeze-frame of that final scene, some more words pop up.

Boo's mini-dorm is unusual, imaginative and wonderful.
Just like Boo.

"That's great. Really great!" I say. "I mean both of you, not just Granny Viv's filming. I mean, Boo, look at all this stuff. You should be proud of your—"

PLING! comes the sound of a message and a text box opens on the screen of my gran's phone.

"Ooh! It's from my dad..." Boo exclaims, just as Granny Viv grabs the phone away.

My gran frowns as she studies the text, then her face breaks into a red crescent of a smile.

"Well, Boo," she says, turning the phone back around so we can see the message for ourselves, "I literally JUST sent this film to your parents and look what's come back!"

Boudicca's mother and I have watched the film.
We've decided to leave Boudicca at the school
for now. We will review the situation in a few
weeks.

WOW! Coming from Boo's dad – who has less
personality than the statue of St Grizzle – that is
a HUGE success. My genius Granny Viv strikes
again, ticking off No. 3 on my **Wrongs to Put
Right List** without even knowing it existed!

I'm guessing Lulu was in on this, as she'd have
had to give Granny Viv the okay to have the
Featherton-Snipes' contact details. But I guess
it's like Lulu and the Beatles say – sometimes you
need a little help from your friends. And it's
better still if that friend is your very own gran...

"Well, THIS calls for a celebration!" announces
Granny Viv, jumping up after squeezing the
breath out of both of us with sheer happiness.

"What are we going to do?" I ask, as me and
Boo scrabble to our feet.

"Why, CONGA, of course! Come on, grab hold!"

And so I put my hands on Granny Viv's waist, and Boo puts her hands on mine, and next thing we know, Zed is grabbing hold of the back of Boo's T-shirt while Stella pushes *him* and a row of shrieking clown Newts cling on to *her*.

"Wait for us!" I'm pleasantly surprised to hear Kyle yell, as he and Abi and Mason merrily muscle into the line.

And on and on it breathlessly goes, a great, giant, laughing, singing, dancing conga line of Grizzlers and Twits, teachers and parents and Lodge residents, mayors and head teachers (I spotted Lulu just dragging Mr Puddock into the line, not taking no for an answer).

We all swirl and whirl out of the clearing and around the back lawn till we're deliciously dizzy. And then Eric launches into an Elvis tune and we're all off again!

But hold on ... there's a bit of a problem with all this fun. With the whole of St Grizzle's joining in, it means no one is on snooping and security duty.

And I've just spotted a glint of white and some jerky movements out of the corner of my eye.

Trapped in the conga line, it takes a few quick turns and spins of my head to see what's going on over by the corner of the building.

It's a solo Spencer, trying to ram Toshio's headphones on to Twinkle's horns!

Twinkle is wriggling from his grasp, but Spencer grits his teeth, looking determined to make it happen.

Till a swooping pigeon dive-bombs him. Super-Marvin!

Squealing, Spencer spins round, flapping his hands above his head and stamping his feet like a two-year-old in the middle of a temper tantrum.

With his back momentarily turned on Twinkle, our amazing goat seizes her chance, lowers her head and goes charging at Spencer's bottom – so hard he disappears completely out of view round the side of the school.

Oh, to have been able to catch that wonderful moment on film!

"Hey, Dani!" I hear Granny Viv call out to me from the front of the conga line. "Getting quite good at this, aren't I?"

Still dancing, she holds up her mobile phone, and quickly presses 'play' on the screen, showing me the very special moment she's just captured.

Genius.

I give my unique Granny Viv a big squeeze round the waist and dance on with everyone in the shadow of the wonderful St Grizzle's School, where guests – as long as they're not pesky – are *always* welcome...

Karen McCombie

Karen McCombie is the best-selling author of a gazillion* books for children, tweens and teens, including series such as the much-loved 'Ally's World' and gently bonkers 'You, Me and Thing', plus novels *Catching Falling Stars* and *The Pearl in the Attic*.

Born in Scotland, Karen now lives in north London with her very Scottish husband Tom, sunshiney daughter Milly and beautiful but bitey cat Dizzy.

Karen loves her job, but is a complete fidget. She regularly packs up her laptop and leaves Office No. 1 (her weeny back bedroom) and has a brisk walk to Office No. 2 (the local garden centre café).

Her hobbies are stroking random cats in the street, smiling at dogs and eating crisps.

You can find her waffling about books, cats and bits & bobs at…

www.karenmccombie.com
Facebook: KarenMcCombieAuthor
Instagram: @karenmccombie
Twitter: @KarenMcCombie

*Okay, more than 80, if you're going to get technical.

Author
Factfile

- **Favourite thing about being an author:**
  Ooh, doing school visits, where I can meet lovely real people, instead of staring at wordies on a computer all day.

- **Second most favourite thing about being an author:**
  Eating cake while I'm writing at Office No. 2 (i.e. my local garden centre café).

- **Best question ever asked during an event:**
  "What's your favourite flavour of crisps?"
  (My answer was ALL crisps are good crisps, but ready salted will always win my heart...)

- **Tell us a secret!**
  Early on at school, I was rubbish at reading and writing because of an undiagnosed hearing problem. From the age of five to six, I basically sat in class wondering what on earth was going on around me. It took an operation and a lot of catching up before I learned to read and write well.

- **Favourite waste of time:**
  Dancing whenever I get the chance, much to my daughter's shame (like THAT'S going to stop me!).

Becka Moor

Becka Moor is an illustrator/author from Manchester, where they say things like 'innit' and 'that's mint, that' when something is really good. She managed to escape the North for a couple of years and ended up in Wales (which, as it happened, was still up North) where she studied Illustration for Children's Publishing at Glyndwr University. Since moving back home, Becka has set up shop in a little home office where she works on all kinds of children's books, including the 'Violet and the Pearl of the Orient' series and *The Three Ninja Pigs* picture book. When she's not hunched over a drawing or pondering which texture to apply to a dragon poo, she can be found chasing her two cats around the house begging for cuddles, or generally making a mess.

You can find more useless information in these dark corners of the interwebs:

www.beckamoor.com
Twitter: @BeckaMoor
Blog: www.becka-moor.tumblr.com

Illustrator Factfile

- **Favourite thing about being an illustrator:**
  Drawing all day!
- **Second most favourite thing about being an illustrator:**
  Getting to read lots of brilliant stories and imagining
  how the characters might look.
- **Tell us something odd!**
  I have a mug collection so huge that the whole world
  could come to my house for tea at the same time, but
  someone else would have to provide the biscuits!
  I'll have a Hobnob or five, please.
- **Favourite waste of time:**
  Baking. It's only a waste of time because I can't bake and
  whatever comes out of the oven is usually inedible!

Find out how Dani first ends up at St Grizzle's in...

GRIZZLE'S
ST ~~GRIZELDA'S~~
SCHOOL
FOR GIRLS,
GOATS AND
RANDOM BOYS

KAREN McCOMBIE

ILLUSTRATED BY BECKA MOOR

My mum loves penguins' bums more than me. Otherwise she'd never dump me in some stuffy old school while she heads off to the Antarctic.

And it gets worse. When we arrive at St Grizelda's School for Girls, the school's had a drastic makeover. Gone are the uniforms, the rules and ... er, most of the pupils and staff. In their place is TOTAL CHAOS.

We're greeted by a bunch of stampeding eight-year-olds, a head-butting goat and a crazy head teacher wearing a plastic-spoon crown.

Somebody get me OUT of here!

KAREN McCOMBIE

ST GRIZZLE'S
SCHOOL
FOR GIRLS,
GHOSTS AND
RUNAWAY GRANNIES

ILLUSTRATED BY BECKA MOOR

GRIZZLE'S

ST ~~GRIZELDA'S~~

SCHOOL
FOR GIRLS,

GEEKS AND
TAG-ALONG ZOMBIES

KAREN McCOMBIE

ILLUSTRATED BY BECKA MOOR

PROPERTY OF
ST GRIZELDA'S
SCHOOL FOR GIRLS